Also by the Author

Blackout

The Erin O'Reilly Mysteries
Book Seventeen

Steven Henry

Clickworks Press • Baltimore, MD

First publication: Clickworks Press, 2022
Release: CWP-EOR17-INT-P.IS-1.0

Sign up for updates, deals, and exclusive sneak peeks at clickworkspress.com/join.

Ebook ISBN: 1-943383-96-2
Paperback ISBN: 978-1-943383-97-8
Hardcover ISBN: 1-943383-98-6

For Susan Roosenraad,
the best high school math teacher
I could ever have hoped for.

Blackout

1. A failure of electrical power supply.
2. Memory loss due to alcohol or drug abuse.

Chapter 1

There was pain, a heavy throbbing behind closed eyelids. With every beat of her pulse, more pain swelled in her head. That was all; no thoughts, no sense of time or space.

She lay where she was, reluctant to move. There was a dull sense, an impression that movement might make the pain worse. So she stayed still. But gradually, in increments, she started to wake up. The head was the worst pain, but her shoulder hurt, too. The sensation was almost like a burn. The whole shoulder felt flushed and raw, rubbing against her blouse.

She became aware of a strange buzzing sensation at her hip. It was insistent, annoying. And something cold and wet was rubbing against her hand. The cold damp was what brought her back to full consciousness. She curled her hand around the furry head that belonged to the wet nose. She felt a pair of very large, perky ears.

"Okay," she muttered. Her tongue felt swollen and the word came out mumbled. That buzzing was still going at her hip. She opened her eyes.

She stared into a pair of intense brown eyes only a few inches from her own. A rhythmic panting was audible. Then her vision was momentarily blocked by a pink, slobbery tongue that swept up across her face.

The thing at her hip kept buzzing. She muttered an oath and fumbled it out of her hip pocket. Swiping her thumb across the screen, she brought the phone up to her ear.

"O'Reilly," she said thickly.

"Where the hell are you?" a voice demanded. It was at least thirty decibels too loud.

Erin O'Reilly blinked and tried to focus her eyes on her surroundings. Where was she? She couldn't remember getting here. The events of the last few hours were a blank.

"I don't know," she said after a moment.

There was a brief pause. "Okay, that's my mistake," said the voice on the phone. "I didn't ask the right question. Fact is, I don't actually care where you are. What I want to know, well, what the Lieutenant wants to know, is why you're not where you're supposed to be. Wanna know how I know you're not there? Because I'm there and you're not."

"Vic?" she guessed.

"You okay, Erin?" Vic Neshenko asked. "You sound kinda funny."

"Yeah. I'm fine. I think."

"Color me unconvinced. Do a vitals check for me. I already know you're breathing, or you wouldn't be talking. You got a pulse?"

Erin forced herself to a sitting position. Her headache spiked. She put a hand to her forehead and felt the blood rushing under her fingertips. "Yeah," she said. "Unfortunately."

"Okay. That means you're alive. And that means you need to, and I quote, 'Get your ass behind your desk before I plant my boot up it.' That's Lieutenant Webb's boot, and your ass he'll be planting it up. If you're confused."

"Thanks for clearing that up, Vic." Erin felt another nudge at her elbow and looked down at Rolf, her German Shepherd K-9. The dog was obviously worried about her.

"Care to give me an ETA I can give Webb?" Vic asked.

"Just a sec." Erin glanced around. She was sitting up on a sofa, a blanket wrapped around her legs. The couch looked vaguely familiar, but the living room wasn't one she knew well. Maybe she'd been there before, but she couldn't be sure. Where on Earth was she? And why couldn't she remember? She saw a glass coffee table in front of her. On it lay a gold detective's shield with the numbers 4640 emblazoned on it. Next to the shield rested a pair of holstered handguns; a Glock automatic and a snub-nosed revolver. She also saw a couple of candles, burned down to stubs. A faint aroma of perfume lingered in the air.

"Erin?" Vic had sounded amused. Now he sounded a little worried. "You sure you're okay?"

"I think so," she said. "I just need to figure out what happened." Her shoulder really felt funny. She rubbed it gingerly.

"Yeah, it was kind of a crazy night for all of us," he said. "I was handling a big pileup on Fifth Avenue half the night. You run into any serious trouble?"

"That's a really good question." There was a sudden silence, and in that silence she realized there'd been a background noise that had been going on since she'd woken up. Running water. It had just stopped.

Erin turned her head toward the hallway and saw a door standing ajar. Little curls of steam were wafting out around it.

"I'll get back to you, Vic," she said quietly. "Somebody's here."

"Erin? What do you mean?" Vic's worry had turned to alarm. "You need backup?"

"Call you back," she said and hung up. She got off the couch, letting the blanket fall to the floor. She'd slept in her clothes, apparently. Her bare feet sank into deep, comfortable carpet. She reached down and picked up her Glock, sliding it out of its holster. Out of habit and training, she pulled back the slide and checked the chamber. It was loaded, a nine-millimeter hollow-point poised and ready to fire.

"*Fuss,*" she murmured, giving Rolf his "heel" command in his native German. Then she advanced across the living room, pistol held in a two-handed grip. The dog stayed at her hip, watching her. He'd picked up on the tension in her voice. His hackles had risen. Though his tail was wagging, it was the furthest thing from friendliness. It was the anticipation of violence.

Erin reached the door. She heard a male voice, a pleasant tenor, somewhat familiar, softly singing. It had a distinctive Irish lilt.

> *"In a neat little town they call Belfast,*
> *Apprentice to trade I was bound,*
> *And many an hour's sweet happiness*
> *I spent in that neat little town.*
> *'Til a great misfortune came o'er me,*
> *And caused me to stray from the land,*
> *Far away from my friends and relations*
> *To follow the black velvet band."*

She put out a foot and shoved the door open, leveling her Glock. "NYPD," she said. "Hands in the air!"

The bathroom air was hot and heavy with clouds of steam. Through the mist, Erin saw a slender man, pale-skinned and red-headed, a spray of freckles across his shoulders. On one shoulder was an intricate Celtic tattoo. He was staring at her with very bright green eyes that showed no fear at all, just a mixture of surprise and mischief. His hands were down at his waist, holding a bath towel. Not counting the towel, he was completely naked.

"And a good morning to you too, love," he said, breaking off his song. "I hope the gun in your hand means you're pleased to see me. I'd love to do as you ask, but if I put my hands up, you'll be getting quite the eyeful."

Erin's aching head spun. "Corky?" she exclaimed. "What in God's name are you doing?"

Chapter 2

James Corcoran gave Erin a megawatt smile. "I'm taking a shower, love. In the washroom, which is the customary place, so I'm told."

"Not that!" she snapped, trying to ignore the man's nudity. "I mean, what are you doing here?"

He blinked. "This is my flat, love. I live here."

"Oh. What am I doing here?"

"Would you mind pointing your revolver elsewhere?" he said, tying the towel around his waist. "You can clearly see I'm unarmed. Though if you'd care to pat me down...?"

"No, thanks." She lowered the Glock. "So, I'm at your apartment. No wonder it looked familiar."

"I don't recall bringing you home with me before," Corky said. "Sadly, our affair never got so far. Besides, I'd have taken you to my other flat in that case."

"I came here last year," she reminded him. "When Carlyle was hiding out from that German hitman."

"Oh, of course! I'd forgotten."

Now Erin knew where she was. But she still didn't know why. "Look, Corky," she said. "I have to go. I guess I overslept and I'm late for work. Just tell me what happened last night and I'll get out of your hair."

"You truly don't know, love? Some lads might find that a mite insulting. I'd hoped I was more memorable than that."

Erin fought down a jolt of pure horror. "You don't mean... we didn't..."

Corky held his poker face as long as he could, but it dissolved into laughter. "Nay, love. Your virtue's as intact as it was before crossing my threshold, and there's not many lasses can say that. But I had to see the look on your face. You should've seen yourself. Eyes like great saucer plates, they were."

Annoyance and relief rushed through her in equal parts. "I'm in a hurry," she said.

"Very well." He took a bathrobe off its hook and swept it around his shoulders. "We were at the Corner, having a few drinks."

"We?" she prompted.

"You, myself, and a few of the lads."

"Carlyle?"

He gave her an odd look. "Nay, love. He's in Chicago with Kyle Finnegan, seeing to business. Don't you recall?"

"Oh. Right." Now that he said it, Erin did remember. Her boyfriend had gone out of town for a few days.

"I was looking after you," Corky went on. "And you did want looking after. I don't know what got into you, but you were drinking the lads right under the table. I don't mind telling you, I was impressed. Not many can match me shot for shot. And then there was the tattoo."

"The *what*?"

He blinked. "Are you feeling quite all right, love? The whole thing was your idea. Though I'll admit you'd a fair few drinks in you by then. I know a lad down the way, a right wizard with the ink, and I'm not one to deny a lass, so I took you there. You were under the needle quite some time."

Erin touched her shoulder again. "Dear Lord," she muttered. "What was the design?"

"You went for a fine, traditional pattern," he said. "Rather like my own, come to that. A Celtic knot, about the size of a golf ball."

"It feels bigger," she said. Her shoulder felt inflamed.

"The lad did fine work," Corky said. "Though I'll admit he was painting on a grand canvas to begin with. It's fortunate he was nearly done when the lights went out."

"I passed out?"

He shook his head. "I'm not being metaphorical, love. The power went down. Not just in the Corner, either. All over Manhattan. Worst blackout I've seen."

"So how did we end up here?"

He grinned. "I took you back to your flat first. Carlyle's got a lovely security system. State of the bloody art. Only one wee problem with it. His door's electrically locked, and there's no sense in it opening if the power goes down. In that case, if a lad wanted to break in, all he'd have to do would be cut the cable. So that fine steel door to his flat won't open for love nor money once the current stops flowing."

Erin put a hand to her face. "I couldn't get my door open," she sighed.

"We waited a wee spell, to see if the power came back," he said. "But after a few minutes, some of the lads downstairs started getting a mite restless. And I did promise Cars you'd be in good hands while he was away, so I thought the best thing was to bring you back here till it all blew over."

"Through the middle of a New York blackout? Was that safe?"

"Of course not," he said cheerfully. "It's a pity you don't remember the adventures we had on the darkened streets. You thought you'd best be going in to work, as your lads would be needing all hands on deck, but I could tell you were sailing a few sheets to the wind, so I talked you out of it."

"Thanks," she said, meaning it. Showing up for work blind drunk wouldn't have done anyone any good.

"In the end, we got here," he said. "I'll have to take my car into the shop to take care of that wee fender-bender, and it's lucky my head was harder than that lad's outside, but no real harm done. I lit some candles, fetched a bottle from my private supply, and we shared it between us. Then your personal lights went out. I'd have given you the bed and slept on the couch myself, but you were already laid out on it and... well, love, there's no way to put this delicately. My back's not what it was, so I thought it best to leave you here."

"Are you making a crack about my weight?" Erin bristled. She was five-foot-six and kept herself in excellent shape. Corky wasn't particularly large or muscular, however, so he might have a point. Dead-weight human bodies were surprisingly hard to shift.

He held up his hands. "Cars would have my head if he heard I was taking liberties with his lass," he said. "Better all 'round not to be manhandling you."

"And that was all that happened?" she pressed, giving him a hard stare.

"What is it you're wanting me to say? You woke up fully clothed, in a separate room from me. And I'm not keen on your implication if you're suggesting I'd take advantage of an unconscious lass. I've never had a girl who wasn't ready and willing."

"I'll bet," she muttered. "Thanks, I guess. But it sounds like we took your car here."

"You were in no condition to drive."

"Why was I drinking so much?" she asked.

He shrugged. "That's between you, your liver, and the Almighty, love. If you don't recall, how can you expect it of me? I'll give you a lift back to the Corner."

"Didn't you just say your car needed to go into the shop?"

"Aye, but it's mostly cosmetic. We only caught a wee piece of that other scunner going through the intersection. The traffic lights went out, too, you ken, so it was a mite exciting, particularly that bit where I had to drive on the sidewalk to avoid the donnybrook in that intersection."

Erin raised an eyebrow, waiting for details that didn't come. Her head hurt too much to press him hard. After a beat, she said, "I'll call a cab."

*   *   *

By the time Erin and Rolf were able to get a taxi, make a quick change of clothing at home, and retrieve Erin's Charger, they were almost two hours late to the Precinct 8 station house. Erin knew she was going to get chewed out. She could feel herself hunching her shoulders in anticipation as she climbed the stairs to the Major Crimes office.

It didn't help that she knew she deserved what she had coming. She'd been good about her drinking the past few months, considering. It hadn't always been easy, especially after her close call with the Italian Mafia. She'd nearly fallen into a deep, dark place that night in New Jersey and the memory still gave her a twinge of shame when she thought about it. She'd failed to take down a big-shot Mafioso, and in the process she'd gone right to the edge of losing herself. That was coupled with the unrelenting strain of an undercover assignment that had been going on far too long, together with her sister-in-law's kidnapping, several dangerous personal encounters, a few gunfights, a bad concussion, and the baseline stress that came with wearing a gold shield.

But going on a bender with James Corcoran for a chaperone went right past foolish into the realm of reckless stupidity. She was lucky Corky had been more responsible than he liked to act, or she could've gotten in real trouble. But Corky had been different ever since the incident with Michelle O'Reilly and Mickey Connor back in June. He'd been chastened and almost pitifully anxious to prove himself to Erin.

She thrust Corky to the back of her mind, where he belonged, and got ready to face the music.

"Look who's here," Vic said when she and Rolf trooped in. Vic looked like Erin felt. He had dark shadows under his eyes and the gaunt, drained look of a man who'd been up all night. Lieutenant Webb, years older and in worse shape to begin with, looked even worse. The Lieutenant had a cup of coffee on his desk and it was definitely not his first. Vic's workstation sported a mostly-empty green bottle that had started the day with two liters of Mountain Dew in it.

"You okay, O'Reilly?" Webb asked.

"Yes, sir," she said. "Sorry for being out of touch."

"I was worried about you," he said. "Thought maybe you'd been abducted or murdered."

"Not yet, sir."

"Good. Then have a seat and get to work."

Erin felt relief so great it was almost a let-down. "That's it?" she couldn't resist asking.

Webb raised an eyebrow. "Of course it isn't. You're two hours past roll call, visibly hung over. I'm giving you a rip, obviously, but if you want me to read you the riot act right now, I'd be happy to oblige. I'm too tired to shout, so I thought I'd give it a couple hours first. You got a problem with that?"

"No, sir." She sat down, her ears burning. Rolf settled beside her desk in his usual spot and gave her a mournful look.

"Anything to report from your blackout?" Webb asked.

She started, then realized he was talking about the power outage. "Nothing major, sir," she said.

"Good," Webb said again. "It looks like most of what came our way was petty crime. Vandalism, some looting. But I think we can expect a few major incidents once they work their way through the pipeline from Patrol."

"Civilization is always four missed meals and one power outage away from the Dark Ages," Vic said balefully.

"I don't think we've got the barbarian hordes outside just yet," Webb said. "The outage only lasted three hours."

"Any idea what caused it?" Erin asked.

"I'll bet Homeland Security's talking to Con Ed right now," Webb said. "I haven't heard anything about a possible terrorist attack or sabotage, but you never know."

"If it's terrorism, that'll go Federal," Vic predicted. "But I bet it was just some idiot who dropped a wrench in the wrong place."

"I think it might take more than that to knock out the power for half of New York City," Webb said.

"You'd be surprised," Vic said. "A guy dropping a wrench in Arkansas blew up a nuclear missile silo once."

"Really?" Erin asked.

"You think I'd make something like that up?" Vic retorted. "I'm dead serious. The wrench knocked a hole in a Titan II's fuel tank. The silo filled with rocket fuel over the next couple hours. Real nasty stuff, caustic, poisonous, explosive. All it needed was a spark, and the whole place went like a bomb. Killed two people. At least the nuke didn't go off. Now *that* would've been something."

"Excuse me."

All heads swiveled toward the stairwell at the sound of the new voice. A young man was standing there, dressed in a spotless white shirt and black slacks. A dark crimson necktie was knotted perfectly around his throat. His dark hair was neatly combed, his smooth, handsome face clean-shaven.

"Jehovah's Witness," Vic guessed under his breath.

"They come in pairs," Erin said out of the side of her mouth.

"Maybe the other one's dead," Vic suggested.

"What can I do for you?" Webb asked, ignoring his detectives.

"I'd like to report a crime," the young man said. "The desk sergeant told me to come up here."

"Okay," Webb said. "Come on in. What's your name?"

"Christopher Millhouse," the young man said. "I'm nineteen years old. I'm a sophomore at Columbia."

Webb nodded. "What's the crime?" he asked.

"Murder."

Erin had her notepad out and was writing down what the kid was saying. She paused and looked up at him. Millhouse appeared completely calm and collected, not at all the way she'd expect a teenager to react if he'd witnessed a killing.

"I see," Webb said. It was obvious he hadn't decided whether to take this kid seriously. "When did this murder take place?"

"Last night. About ten-thirty."

"During the power outage?" Webb asked.

"That's correct," Millhouse said.

"Where did it happen?"

"At a construction project at 133 Greenwich."

"Who was killed?"

"A woman."

"Did you see it happen?"

"Yes."

"You watched the murder being committed?" Webb pressed, leaning forward.

"Not exactly."

"What do you mean?"

Millhouse smiled slightly. Erin had been around a lot of violent, dangerous men during her career. She'd faced down psychopaths, murderers, and gangsters. But that smile on Christopher Millhouse's face was one of the most unsettling things she'd ever seen.

"I killed her," he said.

Chapter 3

Erin had her doubts. False confessions were a common occurrence in a detective's workday. But the look on Millhouse's face had put her on her guard. She stared at him, trying to read deeper into the young man.

Webb was unimpressed. He nodded to Vic, who picked up a phone to direct a Patrol unit to the site. The Lieutenant was also watching Millhouse.

"Why did you kill her?" he asked.

Millhouse shrugged. "I wanted to see what it felt like."

"What's your relationship to the victim?" Erin asked.

"None whatsoever," Millhouse said, still smiling that bland, creepy smile.

"How did you do it?" Webb asked. In the background, Vic was talking to Dispatch, explaining the situation.

"I hit her on the head with a metal rod," Millhouse said calmly. "I think it was a piece of concrete rebar. It had a threaded texture. I suppose it would have left marks on my hands, but I was wearing gloves. She fell down, but she was still alive. She was looking at me, trying to say something. So I pressed the rod across her neck and held it there until she died."

Erin suppressed a shudder. She wished she'd gotten a cup of coffee before this weird kid had shown up. Her head was really pounding.

"Did you plan this ahead of time?" Webb asked.

Millhouse shrugged again. "Not particularly. But I'd been intending to kill someone for a long time. Maybe I always wanted to."

"How did you choose your victim?" Webb asked.

"It seemed like a good idea at the time."

"Why a woman?" Erin asked.

Millhouse looked at her. "Why not?" he replied. Then, almost as an afterthought, he added, "It was a lot easier than I thought it would be."

"What did you do with the body?" she asked.

"Nothing. It's still there."

Webb stood up. "We're going to have to hold you, Mr. Millhouse, while we check your story," he said. "Turn around and place your hands against the wall."

Erin and Rolf moved to back Webb up, just in case Millhouse made any trouble, but the kid quietly obeyed. He offered no resistance as Webb read him his rights and checked his pockets, finding a cell phone, a wallet, and a set of keys.

"Take him downstairs and book him," Webb told Erin.

She steered Millhouse to the elevator, keeping a sharp eye on him. She'd handled dozens of handcuffed perps, but it always paid to be on your guard in close proximity to criminals. You never knew when they might do something unpredictable, and this guy struck her as crazier than most. She made sure to stay behind him and out of his field of view.

He stood quietly all the way down, watching placidly while Erin went through the familiar routine of fingerprinting and mug shots. He kept smiling. That smile was really starting to get on her nerves.

She couldn't help herself. After she got him safely stowed in a holding cell, she paused outside the bars. "Does it bother you?" she asked. "What you did?"

"Not particularly," he said.

"Then why did you come here?"

His smile widened. "You'll see," he said.

*   *   *

"Friggin' psychos," Erin said, half to herself, as she and Rolf returned to Major Crimes. Vic was standing at Webb's desk. Both men looked unhappy.

"No corpse," Vic said. "We've got two units on scene. They say there's no sign of a dead woman. Or a dead man, for that matter."

"Any blood?" she asked.

"Nothing they can see," Webb said. "I can call a CSU team, but we're not even sure if it's a crime scene. I want you to take your K-9 and see if he can sniff out anything. He's trained in search-and-rescue, right?"

"He can sniff out a body," she confirmed.

"Take Neshenko with you," Webb said. "He looks bored, and that makes me nervous. Did our boy lawyer up yet?"

"Not yet," she said. "He seems to think this is all some big joke."

"He's pranking us," Vic said. "We'll get the last laugh when we slap an obstruction of justice charge on him."

Neither Erin nor Webb said anything. Everybody in the room knew that was an unlikely outcome. The New York criminal-justice system had more important things to do than nail a prankster for wasting police time, particularly in the wake of a major power outage. The irony of wasting time on a time-waster wasn't lost on them.

"Whatever," Vic grumbled. "Let's get this over with."

*   *   *

"You got really smashed last night, huh?" Vic said from the passenger seat of Erin's Charger.

"Won't be the last time," she said.

He grinned. "Hey, I've been hammered plenty of times. Good party?"

"It was until the power went out."

"Hey, some parties I've been to, that only makes them better," he said. "Then you can make out with complete strangers in the dark."

"Whatever floats your boat," she said. "Speaking of which, how's it going with you and Zofia?"

"Okay, I guess. I thought maybe the whole pregnancy thing would make her more careful. Maybe she'd ask for a transfer to a desk job or something, I dunno. But I think it's made her a little crazy. She's been working really hard, pulling double shifts all the time, doing all this wacky shit with Logan and his cowboys."

"Makes sense," Erin said. "She knows a time's coming when she won't be able to get around like she can now, so she's living it up while she can." She also remembered how Zofia had hesitated, had frozen in place during a Mob gunfight. She suspected the other woman might be trying to atone, or maybe prove to herself that she still had what it took.

"I guess." Vic wasn't convinced.

"So, you put a ring on her finger yet?"

"Don't even joke about that."

Erin had been only half joking, but she let it be. Vic's relationship with Street Narcotics Enforcement Unit Officer Zofia Piekarski had been complicated lately. Pressuring Vic about it would only make him angry. She wondered how it would all play out.

"You know what the best cure for a hangover is?" Vic asked, changing the subject.

"I swear I've heard every possible one. None of them work. Coffee, raw eggs, whatever. It's all bullshit."

"Fistfight."

"Really? Getting punched in the face cures a hangover? You just made that up."

"I'm serious. Get smacked a couple times, you forget all about the hangover. Then, when the pain from the fight fades, it takes the hangover with it. You don't believe me? Try it."

"Is that your solution to everything? Punch somebody?"

"You'd be surprised how often it works."

"The last time a guy punched me, CSU had to use a hose to get his brains off the ceiling."

Vic opened his mouth, then closed it again. "How's your sister-in-law doing?" he asked in place of whatever he'd been about to say.

"Pretty well, considering." *Considering she was kidnapped, terrorized, and nearly murdered by a sadistic thug*, she thought but didn't add.

"That's good. You really think we're gonna find a body here?"

"I don't know. You think this Millhouse is blowing smoke?"

"I think he's too smooth," Vic said. "Either he's pledging a fraternity or something, trying to get us to chase our own tails, or else something's seriously wrong with him."

"That's what I'm worried about," Erin said. She pointed up ahead, where a pair of NYPD blue-and-whites were parked. "There's the spot."

"Looks like a construction site," Vic said.

"Well, he did say he used rebar," Erin said. She pulled up to the curb.

They found a fenced-off lot with a half-finished foundation. Bags of cement, piles of rebar, and various tools were piled along the inside of the fence. A fancy sign proclaimed that the lot was the future site of Wildfyre, Inc. Corporate Headquarters. Three uniformed officers were standing around, looking bored. Their commander, a Patrol Sergeant, stood at the chain-link gate with her arms crossed. A burly man in an orange vest and hard hat was next to her. He was scowling.

"What've you got?" Erin asked, flashing her shield.

"Oh, good," one of the uniforms said. "The golden boys are here. I guess we can take off."

"Can it, Berkley," the Sergeant said. "If I gotta adjust your attitude again, you'll be walking funny for a week."

Erin smiled thinly, trying to ignore the pounding in her skull. "O'Reilly, Major Crimes," she said. "This is Detective Neshenko."

"Sergeant Neubel," the other woman replied. "I don't know why they bothered sending you guys. There's nothing here."

"No body?" Vic asked.

"No nothing," Neubel said. "We walked the site, found nothing. Got the site foreman here."

"Moe Ledbetter," the foreman said. His scowl dissipated. He gave Erin an appreciative glance, starting at her legs and working his way up. "How ya doin', ma'am?"

"I'd like to take a look inside, sir," she said, ignoring the ogling.

"Me, too." Vic had also noticed the other guy's wandering eyes. He glared at Ledbetter.

"Look all ya want," Ledbetter said. "My guys oughta be working, but the money dried up a few days ago, so the site's dead. You're lucky I was at my other site, just up the way, so's I could get here fast."

He pushed the gate open. "Not much to see," he went on. "It's gonna be a high rise one of these days. God willing. Looks like the idiots I got working for me forgot to lock up last time they left. Any yahoo coulda been wandering around in here. I hope nothing's missing."

Erin was only half listening. She didn't see a corpse, but she hadn't expected to. Sergeant Neubel and the other uniforms would've spotted anything that obvious. Her main purpose was to point Rolf the right direction. She looked down at the K-9, who stared attentively back.

"Rolf, *such!*"

The K-9 sprang into action and started his search, snuffling eagerly. Erin hadn't given him a particular scent, so he started looking for what he'd been trained to find: explosives and hidden people, living or dead. He hurried forward, tail wagging.

Erin intended to let Rolf take his time with the search. She was completely confident in the dog's nose. He could find a fresh corpse even if it had been buried. A good search dog could find a body under several feet of dirt.

But they'd barely started when Rolf froze mid-sniff. He snorted and shook his head violently from side to side.

"What is it, kiddo?" Erin asked, hurrying forward. Rolf snorted again and pawed at his snout. She got down on one knee next to him, laying a hand on his back. She caught a whiff of chemical smell.

"What's the problem?" Vic asked.

"Some sort of solvent," she said, trying to mask her concern. "He got a good whiff. It's okay, boy. *Sei brav.*"

Rolf wagged his tail weakly and sneezed. He looked up at her with watery eyes, looking mournful the way only a dog could.

Erin turned on Ledbetter. "What kind of chemical crap are you guys using on this site?" she demanded.

He shrugged. "We got all kinds of stuff, lady. It's all totally legal."

"So was asbestos, once upon a time," Vic said darkly. "Shit, I can smell it, too. There's stuff all over the place here. I think that's acetone. Maybe some other stuff."

Erin nodded. If she and Vic could smell the chemicals, she could only imagine what the nasty stuff was doing to Rolf's sensitive nostrils. She saw a big discolored patch by the trash dumpster. It appeared to be leaking out of a steel drum. Now that she looked closely, she could see all kinds of stains and spills.

"This place is one big health and safety violation," she said. "I'd better get Rolf out of here. And us, come to that. I feel like I need a gas mask just standing here."

"Or a hazmat suit," Vic muttered. He'd wandered over to the flat concrete slabs that formed the foundation of the construction. "When were these poured?"

"A week ago," Ledbetter said, glancing at the concrete. "They're plenty solid. Concrete sets up in about a day. Nice and hard." He took another moment to check out Erin's backside.

"Looks like a bust," Vic growled. He stomped on the concrete in frustration.

"Yeah," Erin agreed in disgust. "Let's go, before we all get cancer or start coughing up blood."

Once they got outside the chain-link fence, Rolf's breathing immediately improved. The Shepherd gave one final snort. Then he looked at Erin for further instructions. That was the great thing about dogs, she thought. They never dwelled on the past.

Erin took a last look over her shoulder. Ledbetter was still undressing her with his eyes, not even bothering to hide it.

"Want me to break his legs?" Vic asked in a low voice.

"Don't bother," she said. "There's a million more in New York just like him. You can't break all their legs."

"Not with that defeatist attitude," he said. "C'mon, it'd drum up some business for your brother."

"Junior doesn't like me throwing business his way," she said. Sean O'Reilly Junior was a trauma surgeon at Bellevue Hospital. Their jobs intersected more often than either of them would have liked.

"No body?" Sergeant Neubel asked, joining them.

"You were right," Vic said. "No nothing."

Erin's phone buzzed. She hauled it out and saw Webb's name on the screen. She brought it up to her ear.

"O'Reilly," she said.

"You find our alleged victim?" Webb asked.

"No, sir. If there was a body here, looks like it's gone now."

"That'll keep. We've got bigger fish to fry."

"What is it now?" she asked, feeling a stirring of dread.

"We've got a lead on the power outage," he said. "It was a sabotage job. Looks like somebody managed to load a virus into the power plant's computer system."

"Is that possible? I thought they had all sorts of protection."

"Almost enough protection," Webb said dryly. "We're in contact with Homeland on this. They expect to be able to trace the source of the virus. They've asked for the NYPD to provide personnel for a possible raid. ESU is already on standby, but Agent Johnson wants our team to assist. Apparently he remembers us from the City Center bombing."

"Copy that, sir. Where do you need us?"

"Come back to the Eightball. We'll have the ESU team waiting. Since we don't know where we'll be deploying, we might as well stay at the station until we know."

"On our way, sir." Erin hung up.

Vic raised his eyebrows. "Well?"

"Looks like we're hunting terrorists again," she sighed.

"What about Millhouse?"

"What about him?" she retorted. "He's under lock and key. We'll deal with him later."

Chapter 4

Agent Johnson was waiting at the Eightball when Erin, Vic, and Rolf got to Major Crimes. The Homeland Security man had covered up his usual government-issue suit with a Kevlar vest. He was wearing a Glock 47 automatic pistol openly on his belt. He was talking to Webb, who was also wearing tactical gear. The ESU squad was off to one side, locked, loaded, and impatient.

"Guess we're going to a party," Vic commented. "I better put on my dancing shoes."

"Suit up," Webb said, catching sight of them.

"Where are we going, sir?" Erin asked. She grabbed a vest from the equipment locker and strapped it on, then started dressing Rolf in his K-9 body armor. Vic was putting on his own protection.

"We should know in a few minutes," Johnson said. "Good to see you again, O'Reilly, Neshenko. Wish it was under better circumstances."

"What're we dealing with here?" Vic asked. "Al Qaeda? Far-right loonies? Far-left loonies? Plain, ordinary, non-political loonies?"

"Hard to say," Johnson said. "Our hacker knows what he's doing. He masked his IP address. But he also spammed all the major news outlets with his manifesto."

"Could you trace that?" Erin asked.

He shook his head. "No, but we've got a forensic linguistic program running an analysis on the document now. If the author's posted anything else online, we should be able to match it."

"You can do that?" Vic asked, awe and paranoia competing with each other in his voice.

"Every writer has his or her own style," Johnson said. "With a large enough sample size, we should be able to isolate our suspect. Unless he's been really careful in all his online activities, we should have him pegged any moment now."

"That's a little creepy," Erin said.

"It's enormously creepy," Johnson agreed. "But it's also necessary for Homeland to do our job. Remember, we're the good guys."

"If you have to remind people of that, you're not as good as you think," Erin said very quietly. She'd been thinking a lot about the line between heroes and villains lately, and how very blurry that line could get.

"What'd this loser say?" Vic asked.

"He says we're too dependent on modern technology," Johnson said. "He wants people to wake up and start living naturally, without electricity. He says we rely too much on our computers and phones."

"This guy's a hacker, right?" Erin said. "Isn't that a contradiction?"

"He wouldn't be the first extremist to be a hypocrite," Johnson said dryly. "You ever notice the leaders of terrorist movements aren't the ones strapping bombs to themselves?

They're the ones we catch hiding out under false names, using civilians as human shields."

Johnson's phone vibrated. He glanced down at it. "We've got a contact, people!" he said triumphantly. "IP address matched to a user who's online right this minute. If we hurry, we may be able to grab him unaware. He's right here in town!"

The ESU guys grabbed their assault rifles and hustled for the door, the Major Crimes detectives and Agent Johnson right on their heels.

"We taking the Bearcat?" Webb asked the ESU leader, Lieutenant Lewis.

"Copy that," Lewis said. "Where are we going?"

"Columbia campus," Johnson said. "Our boy's in a frat house there."

"I'll call campus security," Webb said. "They tend to get irritated if we cross their turf without giving them a heads-up. And I'll alert Patrol units to form a perimeter."

"Keep them out of sight," Johnson advised. "We don't want to spook the target."

"And an armored car won't spook him?" Erin asked Vic in an undertone.

"When I think low-profile, I think of this," Vic said as they hurried into the parking garage and loaded into the back of the Lenco Bearcat, a hulking black beast of a vehicle. "Hey, Parker. How's it going?"

"Same shit, different day," Parker said.

"You think we need all this hardware to take down some college boy?" Vic asked.

"Remember Charles Whitman?" Parker replied.

"Sounds familiar," Erin said. "But I can't place him."

"University of Texas, 1966," Vic said. "Stabbed his mom and his wife. Then he climbed on top of a tower at the University with a whole lot of guns and ammo. Killed fifteen people before our guys got him."

"The moral of the story is, college campuses aren't safe," Parker said. "Just like everywhere else."

"Our perp launched a deliberate attack on New York City," Lewis said. "We don't know what he's capable of, or what weapons he might have. We got a name on this guy?"

Johnson was looking at his phone, getting information from his tech support. "The room has two students registered," he said. "Royal Forster and Scott Turner."

"Royal Forster?" Vic repeated. "The hell kind of a name is that?"

"Our guy is probably Turner," Johnson went on. "He's a computer science major, blew the lid off his SATs and ACTs."

"You guys really do know everything about everybody," Erin said.

"He's been on our radar," Johnson said.

"Why?" Erin asked.

Johnson didn't immediately answer.

"Because Homeland wanted to recruit him, I expect," Webb said. "Or maybe the NSA or CIA."

"If that were true, it would be classified and I'd have to deny it," Johnson said.

The Bearcat rumbled through the Manhattan streets toward the Columbia campus. It turned onto West 113th, passing a pair of blue-and-whites at the corner.

"Stop here," Lewis told the driver. "We'll go the rest of the way on foot, in case anyone's looking out the windows."

The Bearcat stopped, its engine idling. The ESU team did a final weapon check.

"Okay, team," Lewis said. "Remember, violence of execution. But this isn't Fallujah. It's a frat house. There'll be civilians. We don't know if the target is armed, or if he's got friends. Detain everyone. We'll sort 'em out later."

The ESU team disembarked and started along the sidewalk, moving in tactical formation. Vic, Erin, Webb, Rolf, and Johnson were in the middle of the pack. All the officers had their weapons out and ready. Several students and passersby watched them with open mouths. Cell phone cameras recorded every step of their progress.

They stacked up outside the frat house's front door. By luck, a student was just on his way out. Parker, a big, burly ESU guy, collared the kid.

"What's your name?" he growled, poking the muzzle of his AR-15 into the boy's ribs.

"Jesus Christ!" the kid gasped.

"Wrong answer," Parker said.

"Toby! Toby Frankmuller!"

Parker spun the boy around and frisked him, coming up with a student ID that confirmed his name.

"Where's Scott Turner?" Parker demanded.

"I don't know!" the kid said. His voice cracked a little.

"Which room is his, dumbass?" Parker pressed.

"Upstairs, second floor. Last one at the front of the hall!"

Parker gave Frankmuller a push into the waiting arms of the rest of the ESU team, who promptly zip-tied him and secured him. Then the squad moved inside.

They cleared the first floor with professional speed and skill. They grabbed a pair of boys in the living room who were so engrossed in their game console that they didn't notice the real cops with real guns until Lewis's team was right on top of them. The unit nabbed another guy in the kitchen, knocking the carton of milk out of his hand to spatter white liquid across the linoleum. They hauled him out to join his buddies in the living room, leaving Madsen, one of the ESU guys, to guard the four prisoners.

"First floor clear," Lewis said. "Keep moving, people."

Rolf, at Erin's side, was bouncing on his paws in anticipation. This was definitely the sort of operation that resulted in chasing down bad guys and biting them. It hadn't happened yet, but he was an optimist.

ESU went up the stairs, as focused and tight as if they were storming a drug den instead of a frat house. Two of them peeled off to cover the rest of the upstairs, while Lewis, Parker, Johnson, and the Major Crimes unit went straight to the end. Parker glanced at Lewis, who nodded.

Knocking politely was what police did serving normal warrants. This was a raid on a suspected domestic terrorist. Etiquette went straight out the window. Parker's boot crashed against the door, just below the knob, the kick coming with all the force of his muscular body. The door flew open, spraying a halo of splinters into the air. Parker lunged into the room, Lewis and Vic right on his heels, Erin and Rolf bringing up the rear.

"NYPD! Freeze!" Parker and Vic shouted in near-perfect unison. Erin saw a college dormitory room, festooned with bottles of alcohol and pictures of scantily-clad women. Beside the window, a young man sat at a desk. He was wearing a pair of headphones and had been doing something on a computer. Now he stared at the intruders in stunned shock. He was a good-looking kid, lean and athletic, with wavy black hair and bright blue eyes. Those eyes were wide.

"Hands in the air!" Parker barked. "Get them up! Don't touch that keyboard!"

While Vic covered the kid, Erin scanned the rest of the room. She saw two beds, another computer desk, and a closet. She cleared the closet, making sure no one was hiding behind the hanging clothes. Parker grabbed the student, yanked him out of the chair, and threw him down to the floor. The headphones, ripped from the boy's head, dangled on the end of their cord. Parker planted a knee in the small of the kid's back, wrenched his hands behind him, and cuffed him with brutal efficiency.

"You're hurting me!" the kid gasped breathlessly.

"Clear," Erin reported.

"He's clean," Parker said a moment later, after patting the kid down.

Johnson entered the room and holstered his sidearm. "Agent Johnson, Homeland Security," he said to the boy. "You weren't as clever as you thought, Turner."

The Homeland Security agent paused, taking in the kid's features. He frowned suddenly. "What's your name?" he asked sharply.

"Roy... Roy Forster," the kid said in a tight, strained voice. "Get off me! I didn't do anything!"

"Whose computer is this?" Johnson demanded, bending low over him.

"My roommate's! Scott's! Please!"

"Ease up, Officer," Johnson said to Parker, who stood up.

"Wrong guy?" Vic asked.

"Damn," Johnson said quietly.

Erin glanced out the window. She saw a cluster of students outside the frat house, talking excitedly, and several police officers standing around the front steps. As she looked, she saw a guy at the back of the crowd working his way forward. Suddenly, the young man caught sight of the cops. He stiffened, turned, and started running, shoving his way through his comrades.

"Got him!" Erin snapped. She spun on her heel and sprinted out of the room without further explanation, blowing right past Webb. She went at a dead run, leaving the Lieutenant behind.

One of the ESU guys, Twig, the squad's sniper, caught the urgency in her motion. He came after her, his rifle bouncing on his shoulder.

Erin took the stairs three at a time. Rolf easily kept up, hurling himself down the steps in a furry blur. She jumped the last half flight and hit the floor running. She skidded to a momentary halt, clawed at the doorknob, got it open, and was out the front door, still running flat-out.

"Police! Move!" she shouted at the onlookers, waving her pistol for emphasis. The crowd parted, more from the sight of the onrushing German Shepherd than anything else, and she saw their target, half a block ahead and disappearing around the corner.

"Call it in!" she said over her shoulder to Twig.

"Dispatch!" Twig said into his shoulder radio, timing his words with his breaths. "In pursuit, male suspect, Broadway and 113th. Suspect northbound on Broadway, on foot."

Erin risked a quick look back over her shoulder. Two uniformed officers were trailing them, but they'd been wrong-footed by the suddenness of the chase and one of them had been hitting the donuts and fast food too hard. They were well behind and falling farther back with every stride. It was down to Erin, Rolf, and Twig.

Rolf could outrun anything on two legs, but he didn't yet know who he was chasing. Erin needed a clear line of sight to indicate the K-9's target. Then the Shepherd could show his stuff. But until then, he was dependent on her. He was staying with her, in the absence of orders. His tail lashed excitedly and his tongue flopped out over his teeth. He loved to run more than almost anything.

They reached the corner and turned north on Broadway. Their target still had a good lead. Erin caught a glimpse of him partway up the block. For a computer nerd, the kid could really move. She put her head down and charged ahead, brushing past the intervening pedestrians and blessing her early-morning runs.

"NYPD!" she gasped. "Stop!" But she expected no compliance and got none. It was just part of the procedure, so she could check that box when it came time to write up the report afterward.

The kid still had a lead when they got to 114th. He took a right, heading back toward the campus, probably hoping to lose them in his familiar college haunts. But now he was only about thirty yards ahead, with an open line to Erin and Rolf.

"Rolf, *fass!*" she snapped and let go of his leash.

It was exactly what the K-9 had been hoping to hear. He coiled his powerful legs and hurtled down the sidewalk. Erin was a fast runner, in excellent shape, but the best she could do was about fifteen miles per hour, and that only for short distances. Rolf could double that. He saw only one person running away from him and correctly assumed that was his target.

One of the nicknames cops gave to K-9s was "fur missiles." Rolf homed in on his quarry as if he had radar in his snout, catching up to the kid with no trouble whatsoever. He launched himself the final eight yards with a mighty leap, slamming into the runner teeth-first with all the force of his ninety-pound body. The kid went down and scraped the concrete with his face. Rolf got a mouthful of the kid's windbreaker, which tore free in his jaws. The K-9's momentum carried him clean over the fallen body, tumbling head over tail. He twisted and came up again, spitting out the scrap of fabric and snapping with his jaws.

The kid did the first smart thing he'd done since he'd started running, which was to curl into a ball and cover his head. Rolf did what he'd been trained to do and grabbed his target's right arm, holding on tightly. The boy screamed from fright and pain.

Erin was there seconds later, Twig right behind her. "Don't move!" she shouted. "Don't fight my dog!"

The kid wasn't fighting. He kept screaming, however, right up until Erin and Twig got the cuffs on him and Erin called off her K-9. Rolf sprang back on stiff legs, tail lashing the air, his tongue a long pink streamer in the autumn air. His eyes were alive with happy excitement. He looked for all the world like an overgrown playful puppy out for a walk.

As soon as the boy was securely shackled, Erin fished out Rolf's rubber Kong chew-toy. "*Sei brav,*" she said to him, tossing him the ball. He snagged it in mid-air and chomped down on it, making a wet squeaky sound.

"Dispatch," Twig said, only a little out of breath. "One in custody."

"What'd I do?" the kid on the ground whined.

"Scott Turner?" Erin said.

"Yeah, what? You've got no right to jump me like that!"

Erin and Twig exchanged triumphant looks. "You're under arrest," she told him. "The charge is terrorism."

She saw the realization in his face, coupled with sheer terror, and knew they had the right guy. Feeling almost as much satisfaction as Rolf was taking from his toy, she began the familiar recitation.

"You have the right to remain silent..."

Chapter 5

"Damn," Vic said. "What'd you do to that kid?"

"I didn't do a thing," Erin said. "Rolf started it, the sidewalk finished the job."

They were back at the Eightball, standing in the observation room, staring through the one-way window into the interrogation room. Rolf sat next to Erin, gazing at her with unquestioning devotion and the hope of another round with his chew-toy. Webb and Johnson were sitting on one side of the interrogation table. Scott Turner was on the other.

Vic had a point, Erin had to admit. Turner looked awful. One whole side of his face had been abraded when Rolf had bounced him off the concrete. Now he wore a partial mask of dried blood and scabs. He was a skinny little blond boy who looked very young and very scared.

"Glad he didn't fight back more," Vic said. "You and your mutt might've torn his arms off."

"Last I heard, we don't care what a perp looks like," Erin said, nettled. "Are you forgetting what this jerk did? People could've died. People probably *did* die."

"Yeah, I know," he said. "I just wish he didn't seem like such a..."

Erin waited. "A what?" she asked after a moment.

"Wimp," Vic finished. "I hate beating up on little guys. I always feel like a loser afterward."

"Vic, you're six-foot-three," she reminded him. "Ninety-eight percent of the world are little guys compared to you."

"Is that my fault?"

"Shush," she said, tilting her head toward the window. "They're starting."

In the next room, Agent Johnson leaned forward. He'd be doing the talking. This was a Homeland case. The NYPD were just there to provide logistical support. Webb was in the room primarily as a courtesy and a thank-you for his squad's assistance.

"Scott," Johnson said gently. "Do you know how much trouble you're in here?"

"I didn't do anything," Turner said sulkily. "That bitch's dog *bit* me! I'm going to get rabies or something!"

Erin glanced down at Rolf. It might have been her imagination, but she thought he looked a little indignant at the accusation.

"We've got people going through your computer right now," Johnson said, as if Turner hadn't said anything. "You're good with computers, but they're better. If there's anything on there, they *will* find it. What do you think they're going to find?"

"I'm not the only one who uses it," Turner said. "Roy's on it a lot, too. He could've put anything on there."

"Roy has his own computer," Johnson said, leaving out the fact that Forster had been working on Turner's computer at the very moment ESU had burst in on him.

"But mine's better," Turner said. "It's got twice the processor. Look, I don't know what happened, but he's the guy you want, not me!"

"Weasel," Vic muttered in disgust.

"Didn't take him long to chuck his buddy under the bus," Erin agreed.

Johnson folded his hands on the tabletop and shook his head in mock sadness. "See, here's the problem, Scott," he said. "We've looked into your roommate. Royal Forster isn't exactly a computer whiz. He's a Humanities major who spends his weekends getting drunk and chasing coeds. He plays soccer on the JV squad and will probably make the Varsity team next year. He's a dumb jock who probably thinks a computer virus is something you get from looking at Internet porn if you don't wear gloves when you jerk off."

Vic snorted so hard Erin was afraid he might have injured his nasal passages. Rolf gave him a startled look.

"But you," Johnson went on. "You're taking high-level computer science courses as a sophomore. We've got a file on you at my office. You show tremendous promise as a programmer. You've got books on your bookshelf about computer viruses. See, Scott, even a very good hacker would have trouble taking down New York's power grid. Roy isn't even in that league. But you? You've got the skills."

"I don't have to talk to you," Turner said. "I can ask for a lawyer."

"Of course you can," Johnson said soothingly. "That's your right under the Constitution. But as soon as you do, this will proceed along official channels. Things will start moving that I can't stop, and they'll end with you being put on trial as a domestic terrorist. Federal charges. That means hard time in a Supermax prison. Have you ever heard of Florence Supermax?"

Turner shook his head mutely. His eyes looked like saucer plates.

"It's a prison in Colorado," Johnson explained. "It's where we put domestic terrorists. The Unabomber is there. So is Terry Nichols, the guy who helped Tim McVeigh blow up the Murrow building in Oklahoma City. And Eric Rudolph, you remember him? The Centennial Olympic Park bombing in Atlanta? They call Florence the Alcatraz of the Rockies. It's the most secure prison in the United States. When you're convicted, and believe me, you will be convicted, you'll go into a cell. It's concrete, seven by twelve feet. Just you, twenty-three hours a day, alone with your thoughts. You don't even get a TV until you earn it by good behavior. They'll let you out for an hour in the exercise yard, but it may be at night. You might not see the sun for months at a time. You may get a phone call every now and then, but you've got to earn that, too. And that'll be your life. You understand?"

"Jesus," Erin said quietly. She knew Johnson wasn't exaggerating.

"It'd be kinder if we just took them out and shot them," Vic said. "Nobody ought to live like that."

Turner seemed to agree. Tears were welling up in his eyes. He looked even younger than he had. Erin expected him to start sobbing for his mother any minute.

"That's what'll happen once we get the lawyers involved," Johnson said. "Because you know as well as I do that we've got a good, strong case. I don't want you to go to Supermax, Scott. I don't believe you're a violent psychopath. But you need to help me. I need to understand why you did this, how you did it, and who helped you do it. We got your manifesto, but we both know it's bullshit. So why did you do it, Scott?"

"I just wanted to see if I could," Turner whispered.

"Like climbing a mountain, or going skydiving?" Johnson asked.

"Yeah. It was just supposed to be a joke. Nobody was supposed to get hurt."

"What an ass," Vic growled.

"When you kill the power, more than the lights get turned off," Johnson said. "Refrigerators. Elevators. Life-support systems in hospitals. They've got backup generators, but those take time to turn on. What if somebody's in the middle of having surgery? Or a baby? Or getting a heart transplant? Then there's traffic accidents. Air-traffic control."

"I didn't think," Turner said miserably. He wouldn't look at Johnson or Webb.

"You did plenty of thinking," Johnson said. "You just didn't think about the right things. You had to spend a lot of time planning this. All for a joke?"

Turner shrugged. "It was just a prank," he mumbled.

"Who helped you?"

"Nobody."

"Who knew you were going to do it?"

Another shrug. "I dunno. Maybe some of the guys."

"So this was all over Columbia campus?" Johnson demanded. "And nobody thought to say what a bad idea it was, or to tell somebody in a position of authority?"

Erin frowned. She'd just made a connection she should've made sooner. "Columbia," she said.

"What do you mean?" Vic asked.

"Millhouse," she said. "Our self-confessed killer. He's a Columbia student, too."

"What's that got to do with anything?" he replied. "There's something like six thousand undergrads there. That's like saying two crimes are connected because the perps live in the same neighborhood."

Erin gave him an exasperated look and held it long enough for him to get the message. She hadn't believed in coincidence in years. In the interrogation room, Agent Johnson was pressing Turner for accomplices and getting nowhere.

"Okay, you're right," Vic said. "It's a little weird. But that doesn't mean a thing."

"I'll ask him," she said. "Rolf, *bleib*."

The K-9 obediently stayed where he was, sitting on his haunches, while Erin strode out of the observation room. She went next door and barged right in on the interrogation.

Johnson and Webb both spun to look at her in surprise.

"O'Reilly?" Webb said. "What are you doing?"

"Christopher Millhouse," Erin said, planting her hands on the table and leaning in so she was face-to-face with Turner. "You know him?"

"Chris? Creepy Chris?" Turner was obviously surprised.

"Detective," Johnson said. "I've got this under control."

"So you do know him," she said, ignoring the Homeland Security agent. "Did he help you plan this?"

"What? No!" Turner said. "I don't hang with him. Nobody does!"

"Detective," Johnson said. "I'm conducting this interview. Please leave the room."

"Why do you call him Creepy Chris?" Erin pressed.

"Everybody calls him that!" Turner said. "I've got nothing to do with him!"

"O'Reilly," Webb said quietly, but with a hard edge in his voice. "Agent Johnson isn't in your chain of command and can't give you orders. I am, and I can. Leave the room. Now."

Erin went, fuming. She closed the door to the interrogation room a little harder than strictly necessary. She treated the observation room door even worse, twisting the knob savagely and slamming it shut behind her.

"Take it easy, Erin," Vic said. "You'll bust a blood vessel, ruin your complexion."

"He knows our suspect!" Erin said.

"You mean our alleged suspect for a crime we haven't proved took place?" Vic asked with artificial mildness.

"Shut up. You sound just like Webb."

"I'm just saying what he's going to say. I had an idea, Erin."

"Oh? What's that?"

"Maybe, just for this one case, we could try not pissing the Lieutenant off. Just to mix things up a little. See how it goes. What do you think?"

"I'm wondering who you are, what you did with Vic Neshenko, and why you didn't do it sooner. Now do you want to hear my idea?"

"I'm all ears."

"It looks like Webb and Johnson have this guy wrapped up with a nice bow. Not much left for us to do. So why don't we take a crack at Millhouse and see what he knows about Turner?"

"Why?"

"Because it just occurred to me that he might've come up with the world's weirdest alibi," Erin said. "What if he was Turner's accomplice and knew when things were going down, so he concocted his bullshit story, knowing we couldn't prove it, that'd make us think he was out walking the streets when Turner flipped the switch? That way we wouldn't tie him to the blackout."

"You want my honest opinion?" Vic asked.

"Illuminate me."

"I think it's crap."

"What I love most about you, Vic, is the way you're always so supportive."

He grinned. "You want support, go to group therapy," he said. "I'm not supportive. But I'm intrigued. Let's go talk to Creepy Chris."

*   *   *

They found Christopher Millhouse sitting on the bed in his holding cell. His hands were clasped in his lap. He was humming a tune Erin didn't recognize. She wasn't big on classical music, but thought it might be something by Beethoven.

"How's it going in there, Chris?" she asked.

He deployed that flat, creepy smile across the lower half of his face. "I'm very comfortable, thank you," he said. "How's it going out there? Did you find her?"

"We found Scott Turner," Erin said. "He wasn't as smart as he thought he was. And neither are you. But I'm going to give you a chance to be the smart one. Whichever one of you flips first will get a better deal."

"Detective, I don't think I understand what you're saying," Millhouse said. "I've already given you a full confession. I don't know what more you want from me."

"Listen, you little piss-ant..." Vic began. Erin held up a hand and he fell reluctantly silent.

"Why did you confess?" Erin asked.

"Some people say it's good for the soul," Millhouse said.

"Scott Turner," she said again.

"Is that name supposed to mean something to me?"

"You knew he was planning his little stunt," she said, watching his eyes carefully. "So you made your own plans."

He didn't blink. "Detective, I think you have a problem," he said. "Your department is supposed to be good at catching people who try not to get caught. But here I am, a self-confessed murderer who walked right in your door, and I don't think you can do your job. I think you can hold me for up to forty-eight hours, and after that, I'm going to walk right back out of this cell. And there won't be a thing you can do about it. I will quite literally get away with murder. How does that make you feel?"

Erin studied him. He was trying to make her angry, but what he was doing was making her think. Her headache was nearly gone, thank goodness, and her mind was clearer than it had been earlier.

"You're right that we can only hold you two days without charges," she said. "You've done your homework. Since you've studied the New York legal system, you also know a confession, by itself, isn't enough for a conviction. But it's certainly enough for us to get a search warrant for your home, your computer, your whole life. And if we find anything there, you'll be staring at these bars a lot longer than two days."

That creepy smile was back on Millhouse's face. "If you think I stashed a fresh corpse in my laundry basket, you're free to look," he said. "You seem familiar, Detective. I don't suppose you've been on the news lately?"

Erin said nothing. Her face had been in the *Times* back in June, after she'd shot Mickey Connor. They'd done a whole article. A reporter had tracked her down and tried to get a soundbite. Erin had repeated "no comment" until the guy had gotten the message and left her alone.

"HEROIC DETECTIVE WOUNDED IN DEADLY STANDOFF," Millhouse said, as though reciting something. "I read the article. Your name is... O'Reilly. Erin O'Reilly. You're the one who caught the Heartbreak Killer."

Erin was startled, but tried to cover it up. "That's right," she said. "He thought he was pretty smart, too. But there's always evidence, no matter how hard you try."

"That was good police work, Detective O'Reilly," he said, clapping his hands lightly, almost sarcastically. "It should be very interesting seeing what you turn up. Good luck."

Chapter 6

"He's right," Erin said.

"About what?" Vic retorted. "The guy's friggin' crazy, Erin! He's Looney Tunes! Th-th-th-that's all, folks!"

"It's interesting," she said. They'd retreated to the other side of the security door that sealed off the holding cells from the rest of the station.

"Interesting!" he snorted. "Yeah, the way a bad car crash is interesting."

"Didn't you think it was weird that he knew me?"

"Not really. You've got a rep. You're not exactly anonymous, Erin. You were in the paper for the thing with Connor and for that Heartbreak asshole. Hell, we both made the front page after the City Center last year! I had badge bunnies all over me after that one."

"I don't need to hear about your love life," she said. "But I'm glad it helped you."

"Helped me? Those girls have diseases medical science won't know about for years. I felt like I needed a full-body condom just going out my front door!"

"And that right there crossed over into too much information," she said, making a face. "But that's not my point. Yeah, a lot of guys on the street know who I am. And my face has been in the paper. But he remembered the exact wording of the headline."

"So did you," he said.

"I may get in the news sometimes, but it's not exactly an everyday thing. I remember it when it happens." She sighed and rolled her eyes. "Plus, my mom clips out the articles and mails them to me."

"Really?" Vic grinned. "That's adorable!"

"If I was still living at home, she'd be sticking them to the fridge. But Millhouse isn't family. He'd have no reason to notice something like that. And he started out talking about me shooting Mickey, but that wasn't the important thing to him."

"He went straight to the Heartbreak case," Vic said, nodding. "Like he'd studied it."

"Doesn't that seem a little weird to you?"

"Erin, everything about this guy seems a little weird."

"Point taken. But if he's studying serial-killer cases, I'd call that a red flag."

"Well, that and the fact that he walked into the Eightball saying he'd murdered some chick," Vic said. "Just some random broad he saw walking down the sidewalk."

"No," she said.

"That's what he said," Vic insisted.

"I know he said it. But he was lying."

"So now you think he didn't kill anyone? Then what the hell do we have him in jail for?"

Erin shook her head. "He did *something*," she said. "And for the moment, I'm going to assume he committed a murder last night. Because otherwise this is all just some elaborate practical joke."

"Yeah," Vic said. "Sort of like switching off the power to Manhattan."

"And if he did kill a woman," she went on, "how would he pick her out?"

"Okay, I'll play along," he said. "If he's some sort of budding serial killer, he'll probably have a type. They usually do. So he saw some chick that got him excited and went after her. Not exactly random, but it might as well have been."

"No," she said again. "The power was out, remember? The street would've been awfully dark. Just car headlights, really. And he would've wanted that, to avoid security cameras and eyewitnesses."

"So how did he know who to kill?" Vic wondered. "He must've been following her already, or known her route."

"In which case he knew her, at least by sight," she said. "I'm going to call Judge Ferris and get our warrant. I'm really starting to wonder what this guy has in his bedroom."

"Torture equipment and animal skulls on the wall," Vic predicted. "I'm talking full *Texas Chainsaw Massacre* here."

"Vic, the guy's a nineteen-year-old college student," she said. "He lives in a dormitory. I don't think he's got some poor bastard's face hanging on his bulletin board."

"Maybe not," he said. "But if there's a chainsaw, I get to say 'I told you so.'"

"If he's got a chainsaw in his closet, I'll put ketchup on my shield and eat it," she promised.

*　　*　　*

Judge Ferris was only too happy to sign a warrant for a self-confessed murderer. Armed with the Judge's authority, Erin, Vic, and Rolf climbed into Erin's Charger. She pulled out of the garage and headed back north toward Columbia campus.

"Better let Webb know what we're doing," she said.

"Why me?" Vic asked.

"I'm driving. And I outrank you."

Vic took out his phone and typed a text message. "There," he said. "I told him we were running off to Vegas to get married."

Erin nodded. "Fair enough. Should I get a white dress, or would you like it better if I wore my dress blues?"

He considered that for a moment. "Chicks in uniform are hot," he said.

"Maybe not the best idea," she said. "If I run around Vegas wearing a police dress uniform, won't people assume I'm a stripper?"

"Now there's a thought," Vic said. "You could pick up some extra cash while we're down there. Shake Mommy's little money maker on the Strip, get some twenties in your undies."

"You've got this all planned out, huh?"

"Are you kidding? I don't even know what I'm wearing tomorrow. I don't make plans. You know why?"

"Why?"

"Because the world will break them every damn time. Take Zofia, for instance. What if we'd had this big, complicated plan? Next thing you know, wham! Little baby Neshenko shows up and screws the whole thing. So what's the point? Or this blackout. How many plans you think it messed up?"

"Millhouse had a plan," she said quietly.

"Yeah? How's that working out for him? He's sitting in a jail cell."

"For the moment. And that's part of his plan."

"But we'll find something," Vic said. "I mean, that's what the warrant's for, isn't it?"

"Yeah," Erin said. "But Millhouse is smart. Whatever he's got lying around, it won't make things easy. I think he's yanking us around."

Erin parked in a police spot near the admin offices and went looking for the head of security. Vic thought this was a waste of time, but she insisted.

"It's proper protocol," she said.

"We didn't do it earlier today," he said.

"That was a time-sensitive Homeland Security operation," she reminded him. "That was Agent Johnson's call. The Feds can get away with crap like that. Besides, Webb did call once we were on site."

"I'm sure the campus rent-a-cops will see it your way."

Vic's pessimism proved well founded. The head of campus security was a red-faced, jowly, heavyset man named Oglesby. When he saw them in his doorway, his eyebrows went down in a scowl.

"Mr. Oglesby," Erin said. "My name's Erin O'Reilly. I'm with NYPD Major Crimes. I'm here to—"

That was as far as she got. Oglesby jumped up from his desk, his body quivering with indignation, like an irritable mound of Jell-O.

"Your apology is not accepted!" he shouted. Heads in the outer office turned to see what the fuss was about. Side conversations died into silence.

"Respectfully, sir—" Erin began.

"You people come in here like goddamn storm troopers!" Oglesby roared. "Kicking down doors and dragging students away! We could've taken care of whatever problem you've got, and done it quietly! Discreetly!"

"I can see you're discreet," Vic said, but he said it quietly and Oglesby either didn't hear him or ignored him.

"But no!" the security man went on. "You wanted your photo op, your headlines! You idiots never think about the damage you cause! Now I've got five students missing. Missing! I've got families to deal with! The rest of the student body doesn't know what to think! They're talking about demonstrations! They're mad and they're scared. What'll happen then? You planning on deploying the riot squad? Tear gas? Maybe going full-on Kent State?"

Erin was waiting for Oglesby to run out of breath, but the man seemed to have an inexhaustible supply. She just stood her ground with a neutral expression plastered on her face and let him go. The other option, to have Rolf or Vic take him down, was tempting but not a good idea.

"We have an existing relationship with the NYPD!" Oglesby continued without a pause. "I know you have technical jurisdiction, but you're supposed to go through us! Through channels! I had no idea this raid was going to happen. I still don't know what it's about! Your damn SWAT team drives up in a friggin' tank, right down the middle of the street, in broad daylight! You don't show a warrant, you don't—"

Erin saw her opportunity. Wordlessly, she held out the piece of paper in her hand.

Oglesby snatched it away from her and gave it a contemptuous look. "What am I supposed to do with this, wipe my ass?" he growled. Then he looked a little closer at it and frowned. "You've got the wrong name on this! Christopher Millhouse isn't even in that house! You didn't arrest him!"

"We arrested him earlier this morning, sir," Erin said. "This is an unrelated matter. You'll need to contact Homeland Security for the proper paperwork on the raid. We were operating under their direction."

"You were what?" Oglesby asked, his stream of words finally running dry.

"Homeland Security," she repeated. "One of the young men we detained has already confessed to causing last night's blackout. He's being held as a domestic terrorist."

Oglesby's jaw flapped. His jowls waggled. "Sigma Nu is just a bunch of frat boys," he finally managed to say. "They're harmless."

"As I said, sir, one of them has already confessed," Erin said. "But that's not why Detective Neshenko and I are here today. This warrant is to search Christopher Millhouse's room. If you or one of your officers would escort us there, I'd appreciate it. I'll have to refer your issues with the way the raid was conducted to our Homeland Security liaison. I'll ask him to contact you."

"What does this Millhouse kid have to do with anything?" Oglesby asked.

"It's on the warrant, sir," she said. "He's confessed to murder."

Oglesby, most of the bluster knocked out of him by the words "murder" and "terrorism," was remarkably quiet as he accompanied Erin, Vic, and Rolf to Millhouse's dormitory. Millhouse lived in a two-room suite with an adjoining bathroom, which he shared with three other students. One of the roommates answered Oglesby's knock. He was wearing a bathrobe that hung open to his waist, revealing a pair of boxer shorts. The shorts were adorned with an elephant's face, its trunk hanging in an absurdly suggestive way.

"Whoa," the kid said, taking in the three humans and dog at his door.

Erin held up her shield. "Detective O'Reilly, Major Crimes," she said. "We've got a warrant to search these premises."

Oglesby had examined the paperwork on the walk over. It was completely correct. Judge Ferris had been sitting on the bench over half his very long life. He and his clerks weren't known for making mistakes. Now the security chief held out the warrant.

"Cool," the kid said. "Is that a real gun?"

"No, it's a water pistol," Vic said. "And we got our shields out of cereal boxes. I guess there wasn't much of an entrance exam to get you here, was there?"

"Please show us where Christopher Millhouse's belongings are," Erin said.

The kid, who identified himself as Brady Powers, got out of the way.

"Chris and me, this one's ours," he said, pointing to a pair of desks and twin beds. "I'm on the left."

Erin and Vic already had their disposable gloves on. They started looking through Millhouse's desk, which included a small bookshelf and a laptop computer. Erin unplugged the computer and handed it to Vic. They'd have one of the NYPD's techs look through it later.

"No chainsaws," Erin observed after a few minutes.

"No," Vic said regretfully. The room was divided down the middle by an invisible line. On one side lay piles of wrinkled laundry, discarded candy wrappers, and crumpled pieces of paper. On the other was a neatly made bed and a very tidy desk.

Erin examined the bed. Her own mother couldn't have made sharper corners in the sheet. It would've passed inspection in a Marine barracks. Millhouse's closet held neatly pressed white button-down shirts and black slacks.

"Not much variety in the wardrobe," she said to Vic.

"I bet he uses a lot of this," he said, tapping a big bottle of bleach with his foot. Rolf took a curious sniff at the bottle, snorted, and backed off.

"Tell me about Chris," Erin said to Powers.

"I dunno," Powers said. "He's a little weird, I guess, but he mostly keeps to himself. He's always real polite. Listens to funny music."

"Funny how?" she asked.

He shrugged. "Old stuff. Like, classical. But he uses headphones, so nobody cares much. He reads a lot. Doesn't like us to make a lot of noise."

"What's he studying?" Her attention had gone to his books.

"Psych," Powers said. "I think he wants to be some kind of counselor or something. He was saying something about studying people with problems."

"You mean mental disabilities?"

"Not exactly." Powers wrinkled his nose. "More like psychos. You know, like Hannibal Lecter and stuff."

"*Silence of the Lambs*," Vic said, pointing to the shelf. There was the book, next to another one called *Mindhunter*. Erin recognized the name of the author on that one. John E. Douglas was the FBI agent who had helped create the science of behavior profiling. He'd used it to chase down pattern killers.

"Chris likes serial killers?" she asked.

"Yeah," Powers said. "But that's required reading for one of his classes."

Erin and Vic glanced at each other. "Which one?" they asked in unison.

Chapter 7

"*The Psychology of Psychopaths*," Vic said, shouldering open the door of Schermerhorn Hall. "You think the NYPD might want to keep an eye on the kids who enroll in a class with a name like that?"

"It's a free country, Vic," Erin said. "If we start pulling crap like that, we'll end up being the Thought Police. Haven't you seen *Minority Report*?"

"Yeah, I love that movie."

"But the point of that film is, you can't arrest people for things they might or might not do," she said. She studied the building's directory. "Looks like the Psych Department is up on the fourth floor."

Vic reached for the elevator call button. Erin shook her head and went for the stairs.

"What is it with you and elevators?" he asked, jogging up the steps beside her.

"Ready-made kill-boxes," she said, repeating one of Ian Thompson's personal survival tips.

"Has anyone ever shot at you in an elevator?"

"No, because I take the stairs."

"Has anyone ever shot at you in a stairwell?"

"No, because they're expecting me to take the elevator."

"There is just no reasoning with you."

"Paranoia has its own logic."

They reached the fourth floor just as class was letting out. A wave of students cascaded out of the classrooms and swept around them. The detectives swam against the current, making their way toward the faculty offices.

"Excuse me. You look a little lost," said a middle-aged woman in horn-rimmed glasses that reminded Erin of her grandmother. "May I help you find something?"

"Detective Erin O'Reilly, NYPD Major Crimes," Erin said, flashing her shield. "This is Detective Neshenko. I'm looking for whoever teaches the *Psychology of Psychopaths* class. On your department's website it just says 'Visiting Faculty.'"

The woman's face grew concerned. "Why don't we step into my office?" she suggested.

Erin, Vic, and Rolf followed the woman to an office with the name P. Saunders stenciled on the frosted glass. Erin closed the door behind them. The office was a little cramped for three people and a large dog, and there were only two chairs. Vic leaned against the door. Erin and the other woman sat down. Rolf sat beside Erin.

"I'm Penelope Saunders," the woman said. "Chair of the Psychology Department. You're looking for Annmarie Hilton?"

"Maybe," Erin said. "Is she the one teaching that class?"

"Yes. She's visiting from Berkeley this term. As I'm sure you're aware, Columbia's Psychology Department is ranked in the top twenty in the country, but Berkeley is also extremely highly respected. Professor Hilton is an expert in the field of abnormal psychology."

"Great," Erin said, not caring a bit about Columbia's academic credentials. "Is she in the building right now?"

"I'm afraid not," Professor Saunders said.

"When's she going to be in?"

The troubled look on the professor's face deepened. "That's just the thing, Detective. She should be here right now. One of her classes should have been conducted over the past hour. She didn't show up."

"Did she contact anyone in the Department?" Erin asked.

Professor Saunders shook her head. "Professor Hilton is very professional. When you showed up asking about her, I thought maybe something had happened. But if that were the case, why wouldn't you know her name?"

"We were hoping to talk to her about one of her students," Erin said.

"Oh dear," Professor Saunders said. "Is this about that confusion at Sigma Nu earlier today?"

"We can't comment on that investigation," Erin said. "Did you have any contact with a student named Christopher Millhouse?"

She saw the recognition in the woman's eyes. "Yes," Professor Saunders said. "I met with him just before class registration for this term. He wanted to register for Professor Hilton's class, even though it was intended for Psychology majors and Mr. Millhouse hadn't yet declared his major. He wanted a special exception."

"Did he say why he wanted to take the class?"

"He said he was intending to become a forensic psychologist for the FBI," the professor said. "And this class would look good on his resume when he applied to Quantico."

"He couldn't wait a year?"

"Professor Hilton is only here for this term. She'll be going back to Berkeley once it ends."

"Do you have Ms. Hilton's contact information?" Erin asked.

"Of course." Professor Saunders opened a desk drawer and extracted a spiral notebook, which Erin found amusingly quaint in this digital age. The professor flipped through it, found the page she wanted, and turned it around to show Erin. There, in neat, perfect handwriting, was Annmarie Hilton's name, along with an e-mail address, phone number, and street address. Erin took out her own notepad and copied down the info.

"Why do you guys study psychos here?" Vic asked suddenly.

Professor Saunders gave him a cool look. "That's not a clinical term, Detective," she said.

"Psychopaths," he corrected himself.

"What is a psychopath, Detective?"

"Someone who enjoys hurting people."

The professor shook her head. "That's incorrect, Detective. You're thinking of a sadist. A psychopath is a man or woman with an egocentric, antisocial personality. It's not an official clinical diagnosis, however."

"Really?" Erin asked.

"The DSM-5 recognizes psychopathy as a specifier of antisocial personality disorder," Professor Saunders said. "That's a first in this edition."

"Excuse me," Erin said. "DSM-5?"

"The Diagnostic and Statistical Manual of Mental Disorders, Fifth Edition," the professor explained. "It was published in 2013. Prior to that, we'd be talking about ASPD. Abnormal psychology is an evolving field. Put simply, psychopaths are incapable of experiencing remorse or empathy. They experience very little or no fear or anxiety. Put simply, when they do something wrong, they are incapable of recognizing its wrongness. But most psychopaths are not criminals, at least not in the way you might use the word. They learn to mimic proper social behavior as a survival technique. The most successful psychopaths disguise their nature by studying other people and imitating them. They can laugh at jokes, cry real tears. But it is only an act, a deliberate performance. Many of them are peaceful, productive members of society. Indeed, many of the highest achievers in America are diagnosable as psychopaths. CEOs of corporations; politicians; important and powerful people. Some say their single-minded focus is a strength, rather than a disability."

"And serial killers?" Erin asked.

"Unfortunately, yes," Professor Saunders said. "A small minority. But that is precisely why we need to study such individuals. We can learn to identify them and channel them into constructive pursuits. Ignorance only results in them needing to find their own way in the world, sometimes with tragic results. Detectives, what is this about?"

"We're just trying to build a profile on Christopher Millhouse," Erin said. "Right now we want to know as much as we can about his personality and behavior. How did he strike you when you met with him?"

"He was a very polite, well-mannered young man," Professor Saunders said. "He dressed very neatly and was very controlled and deliberate in his speech."

"Almost like he was playing a role?" Erin asked gently.

The professor looked Erin in the eye. "What did he do?" she asked.

"That's what we're trying to figure out," Erin told her. She stood up. "Thank you for your time, Professor."

She had her hand on the door before the thought struck her. "One more thing," she said. "As a colleague and friend of Annmarie Hilton, you can request the NYPD perform a wellness check. Would you like us to do that?"

"If you wouldn't mind," Professor Saunders said. "It's nice of you to offer."

* * *

"Clever move," Vic said once they were outside the professor's office. "With the prof requesting a wellness check, we won't need a warrant to go into Hilton's place. So our boy's a psychopath?"

"It sure sounds that way," Erin said. "But you heard what she said. That doesn't make him a killer."

"No," he agreed. "But don't you think it's a little too much of a coincidence that his prof went missing overnight?"

"Yeah," Erin said. She already had her phone out and was dialing Professor Hilton's number. It started to ring. After five rings, it rolled over to voicemail.

"Professor Hilton," Erin said after the beep. "This is Detective O'Reilly with the NYPD. I need to talk to you as quickly as possible. It's about one of your students. Please call me back at this number as soon as you get this."

"You're an optimist," Vic said. "I don't think anyone's ever gonna listen to that message."

"I'm afraid not," she said. "But I have to try. Her apartment's just down the street. Let's go check it out."

"Yeah," he said. "Maybe she's just in bed with the flu."

"Maybe," Erin said without conviction.

"Or maybe Millhouse killed her and stashed the body in her own apartment," he went on with ghastly relish. "Maybe he tucked her in bed, put some stuffed animals in there with her…"

"You're a creep," she said.

"I'm just saying, when we get there, we should have your mutt take a sniff under the door. He's good at smelling out corpses, right?"

"Right. But then why would he send us on that wild goose chase to that construction site?"

"I don't know. So we waste time there? Maybe he thinks if he gives us a fake murder story, we won't think he really killed her some other way. I don't know, Erin. I don't think like psychos."

"But we're going to have to," she said. "If we want to figure this out. Let's go."

*   *   *

Annmarie Hilton's apartment was only a couple of blocks from the campus. The detectives got no answer when they buzzed her from the front door.

"I'm starting to think you're right," Vic said. "I think she's dead."

"If she's not, we're wasting time and taxpayer dollars," Erin said.

"I hate wasting taxpayer dollars," he said, hitting the button for the building superintendent. After a minute, the super peered through the glass doors. Erin held up her shield and tapped it against the glass. The man let them in, a surprised look on his face.

"This is a pretty quiet building," he said. "No trouble with gangs, no drugs, no burglaries. What's the problem, officers?"

"We're making a wellness check on one of your residents," Erin said. "Annmarie Hilton, up on Five."

"She didn't answer? Maybe she just stepped out."

"That's what we need to determine, sir. If you'd be so kind?"

The super nodded and, to Erin's discomfort but not surprise, went to the elevator. They rode up to the fifth floor, Erin trying not to be twitchy as she watched the numbers light up. Nobody knew she was coming here, she told herself. Nobody was waiting with a gun. She had to do something about this paranoia. It was driving her nuts.

They reached the fifth floor and stepped into an empty hallway. Erin relaxed slightly. The super went to the door of 505 and knocked.

"Ms. Hilton?" he called.

"NYPD wellness check," Erin said. "Are you in there, ma'am?"

There was no response.

They gave it a minute. Then Erin knocked and called again, louder. There was no sign of life.

She turned to the super. "Open the door, please," she said.

He shrugged and got out his keys. Erin and Vic both rested their hands on their gun butts, just in case. They had no reason to believe trouble was waiting for them, but habits were hard to break, especially the ones that kept you alive.

The door opened onto a sparsely appointed apartment, obviously the sort of place that was rented out fully furnished. The furniture was generic and didn't look too comfortable. Everything was neat and clean.

"Ms. Hilton?" Erin called. "This is the police. Is anyone here?"

She already knew she wouldn't get an answer. Deserted rooms had a particular feel to them that a cop learned to sense. Nobody was here.

"Rolf, *such*," she ordered.

Rolf nosed into the apartment, snuffling his way from one room to the next. Erin and her K-9 cleared the place quickly, finding nobody.

"Got an empty hanger here," Vic reported from the front closet. "Between three other hanging jackets. Probably for the coat she was wearing last night. She's got about a hundred pairs of shoes, so I can't tell if any are missing. What is it with women and shoes? You're a woman, Erin, sort of. Explain it to me."

Erin came out of the bedroom. "It's because we're judged by how we look," she said. "By women and men both. So we try to look as good as possible."

"Hey, not complaining about that," he said. "I like looking at women as much as the next guy."

Erin considered the apartment and the super, who was still standing in the doorway. The wellness check was a good way to sidestep the requirement of obtaining a search warrant, but if they didn't find evidence of a crime at the apartment, they couldn't call in CSU and they couldn't remove things from the premises. Their visit was supposed to be purely aimed at determining whether the resident was alive and in good health. All Erin could tell was that Annmarie Hilton wasn't there. She saw no signs of forced entry, burglary, or any sort of struggle. It was like the woman had just walked out of her own life, intending to come back to it any minute.

"Do you have security cameras?" she asked the super.

"Sure," he said. "One in the lobby."

"Would you have footage from the last couple of days?"

"No problem. We keep a week's worth, just in case." He smiled. "Not that anyone's ever needed to look at them while I've been here."

"Mind if we take a peek?"

He locked up after them and escorted them to his office, where they found an ancient CRT monitor hooked up to a grainy black-and-white camera feed. Erin sat down and started skimming backward, watching the time stamp.

"This'd be easier if we knew what she looked like," Vic commented, looking over her shoulder.

"I assume you've met Ms. Hilton?" Erin asked the super.

"Of course," he said.

"What does she look like?"

"Tall lady, long hair, blonde. Good-looking. Nice eyes. Wears some makeup, but not a lot."

"How does she dress?"

He shrugged. "Like a professional woman, I guess. Skirts that go about to the knee, suit coats, that sort of thing."

"Any jewelry?"

"Necklace and earrings, last I saw." The man smiled. "No wedding ring."

Erin turned to Vic. "This may take a while. Want to step out to the car and run her through the system?"

"Might as well," he said. "Five bucks says she's not in the database."

"You're on," she said, not because she didn't believe him, but because he'd be sure to look that little extra bit harder if money was riding on it.

Vic left the room and Erin went back to looking at the security tape. She saw several women coming and going, but nobody matching the description of Professor Hilton. Suddenly, the screen went black.

"That's the power outage," the super explained.

After a couple of seconds, the tape resumed, the time stamp jumping three hours. Erin saw movement and stabbed the pause button. There, on screen, was a tall woman with long, light-colored hair.

"Is that Annmarie?" she asked.

The super squinted at the screen. "Yeah," he said.

Erin noted the time as 9:58. The power had gone down at ten o'clock sharp. They'd been lucky to catch this glimpse of Annmarie. The woman was dressed for walking. She had on a warm coat. A scarf was wrapped around her neck.

"But you didn't walk all the way down to Greenwich Street," she muttered. "That's half the island. What's going on here?"

Vic returned with a smug smile on his face. "You owe me five bucks," he said. "The NYPD never heard of Annmarie Hilton."

"She's from California," Erin said. "No big surprise."

"She's from California?" the super repeated. "No wonder. She's a babe."

Erin and Vic both looked at him.

"What?" he said. "What'd I say? You guys are just checking in on her, right? I mean, it's not like she did anything. Did she?"

The detectives turned back to the monitor and ignored the man.

"What was she doing so close to the Eightball?" Erin asked. "Assuming it's her."

"That's assuming a lot," Vic said.

Erin laid out the points on her fingers. "She's not at home. She's not answering her phone. Did you see a cell lying around up there?"

"No," he admitted.

"Millhouse knew her," she went on. "She left a couple minutes before the power went down. She didn't come back yet."

"Maybe she got lucky, got laid, and slept over," he suggested.

"Maybe," Erin sighed. "But we can't get her phone records, or look through her correspondence, without a warrant. And we can't get a warrant because we don't have any proof she's our victim."

"That sneaky son of a bitch planned it this way," Vic growled. "He gave us just enough to get us all hot and bothered, then he leaves us hanging. Goddamn tease is what he is. He oughta at least buy us dinner."

"Feeling dirty and used?" she asked, fighting back a smile.

"A little, yeah."

Erin's phone buzzed. She pulled it out and saw the number of one of Carlyle's burners. "Just a second," she said, standing up. "I better take this."

"Speaking of being dirty and used, it's probably your boyfriend," he said with a grin.

Erin stepped out of the office, not wanting to have this conversation in front of a civilian. She took a quick glance around to make sure nobody was in earshot, then answered the phone.

"O'Reilly," she said. It was Carlyle's phone, but she wasn't assuming it was him until she heard his voice.

"Hello, darling," he said in his unmistakable Belfast brogue. "I hope all's well with you."

"Same old, same old," she said. "Where are you?"

"Just about to board the plane at O'Hare. I'll be home this evening."

"Good." Erin's hand shook as she held the phone to her ear and she didn't know why. She was fighting off tears. She didn't understand it and didn't like it.

"What would be your plans for tonight?" he asked.

"I'm planning on seeing you," she said, trying to keep her voice steady. What in God's name was the matter with her?

"I'm hosting a wee get-together at the Corner," he said. "On short notice, I fear. You're invited, of course. Just an evening of cards with some of the lads. We've not had one in a while."

She closed her eyes and clenched her hand around the phone, feeling the edges of the plastic frame dig into her fingers. The very last thing she wanted to do was welcome her boyfriend home in the company of Evan O'Malley and the rest of his gang. They hadn't had one of their periodic poker games since Mickey had been shot. She could only imagine what the rest of the guests were thinking of her.

"Are you there, darling? Your voice sounded a mite odd. I don't know how this connection is."

"I'm here," she said dully. "Yeah, of course I'll be there."

"We're landing a bit after eight," he said. "Finnegan and I will be coming straight there. We'll meet the rest of you with a view to be starting at nine. Can you play hostess until I arrive?"

"Copy that," she said.

"Are you all right, darling? Truly?"

"I'll be fine as soon as you get here," she said. "See you in a few hours."

"Ta, darling." He hung up.

Erin stared at the phone. She'd just figured out why she'd gotten so drunk the night before. It had slipped out in the last thing she'd said to Carlyle. She wasn't fine. And it wasn't because she couldn't live without her boyfriend or any bullshit like that. It was because he'd gone off with Kyle Finnegan, the O'Malley family's resident lunatic, a man who'd beaten three union reps to death with a tire iron outside Detroit, according to underworld gossip. Some part of her had been darkly sure she'd never see him again. The alcohol had been her way of dealing with the stress and uncertainty.

That was silly, of course. If the O'Malleys wanted Carlyle dead, they wouldn't bother flying him all the way to Chicago. Not when they had so many excellent hitmen right here in New York. But fear was rarely rational.

Erin put the phone back in her pocket and swiped the back of her hand across her eyes to take care of any residual moisture. She could handle this. She'd dealt with plenty worse in her career.

But maybe it would be a good idea not to hit the booze when Carlyle was out of town in the future. At least, not unless she wanted another unplanned tattoo.

Chapter 8

Back in the Charger, Erin took out her phone to call Webb. Vic, in the passenger seat, trimmed a fingernail with his tactical knife. Rolf curled up in his compartment and tucked his snout under his tail.

"You got a body for us?" Webb asked by way of greeting.

"Not yet, sir," she said. "But we've got a missing person."

"Who's the lucky one?"

"Annmarie Hilton. She's Millhouse's psych professor."

There was a brief pause. "You think he whacked his teacher?" Webb asked, raising an eyebrow.

"We've got video of her leaving her apartment at the start of the murder window," she said. "She's not answering her phone, she's not home, and she didn't show up for her classes today. That, combined with Millhouse's connection to her, is pretty suspicious."

"I agree," Webb said. "But we can't do much with it. Not without a body, or at least some physical evidence. Where's the apartment?"

"By Columbia."

"That's miles from Greenwich Street," he said. "It'd take her half an hour to get down there."

"She left just before ten," Erin said. "Millhouse claims he killed his target at ten-thirty."

"And we won't have traffic cameras, security cams, or any other electronic surveillance to place either of them there," he said heavily. "Do you know why she'd be that far south?"

"No idea, sir. But I'd like to put out a BOLO for her."

"You think she's dead."

"But I might be wrong, and if she's still alive, I'd like to talk to her about Millhouse."

"Are you sure she's not home? Sick or sleeping, maybe?"

"Vic and I checked the apartment."

"Without a warrant?" Webb asked sharply.

"The department chair requested a wellness check," she said. "At my prompting."

Webb chuckled dryly. "Well played," he said. "Did you happen to notice a daily planner while you were there? Any notebooks? A computer?"

"Without a warrant, we couldn't go through her stuff," Erin said. "You know that, sir."

"Right." Webb sighed. "Damned if we do, damned if we don't. Where are you now?"

"Near the campus."

"Any other leads on our self-confessed killer?"

"Afraid not, sir."

"Then come on back to the Eightball. We're still working through our pitiful little domestic terrorist cell. We're done with Turner, but we're still screening his housemates."

"You think they had anything to do with it?"

"I don't know, O'Reilly. That's why we're talking to them." Webb said it slowly, as though spelling it out to a particularly slow student.

"Copy that, sir," Erin said, keeping her own voice neutral. "On our way."

"Maybe our boy's a cannibal," Vic suggested as they drove. "Maybe that's how he disposed of the body."

"Vic, Millhouse is pretty skinny. He can't weigh over one-sixty dripping wet. Annmarie Hilton looked like she was about five-ten on that camera, which would make her weigh at least as much as he does."

"Your point?"

"My point is, a human being can't eat his own body weight of meat. Even dogs can't do that, not even a hungry boy like Rolf." She reached back into Rolf's compartment and ruffled his fur. The K-9 perked his head up at the word "hungry." Erin often used that word just before giving him food. He'd never had the chance to eat ninety pounds of raw meat, but he'd be willing to give it his best shot.

"And that's not counting the bones," Vic said. "Oh, I know what he used!"

"What?"

"Drain cleaner."

"Would that work?"

"Oh yeah, absolutely. It'll dissolve anything organic, even bones. Takes a few hours, but you could fill a bathtub with the stuff, dump the body in, and pour the whole thing down the drain."

Erin wrinkled her nose. "Okay, leaving aside the fact that you know that, which is creepy, by the way, that frat house didn't have a bathtub. So even if he lugged a fresh corpse halfway across town—on the subway, maybe, I don't know—he wouldn't have a place to dissolve it. And there would've been a smell. Drain cleaner is strong stuff and it's got a distinctive scent. I'm guessing a dissolving body stinks, too. There's easier ways to get rid of bodies."

"We have to find the corpse," Vic said. "Otherwise we've got no case."

"I know that!" she said sharply. "But he didn't dunk her in Drano."

"You seem pretty sure he told the truth about where it happened," he observed.

"Yeah."

"Why?"

"Because he thinks he's smarter than us," she said. "He didn't have to come in at all. This isn't about getting away with murder. He wants us to *know* he's getting away with murder. He's giving us just enough to suspect him, but not enough to prove anything. This is a goddamn game to him. There's no point giving us a specific address unless he's got a good reason. The point is to prove he can kill someone, tell us he did it, tell us when and where, and still walk."

"This kid's a psycho all right," Vic said.

"Yeah, and that's not the worst of it," she said.

"I know. The worst is, if he gets away with it once, he'll do it again. Guaranteed."

"Because it's fun," she said.

"This guy's just like that son of a bitch Heartbreak Killer," he growled.

She shook her head. "No. Those were sex crimes."

"He didn't rape the girls he killed," Vic said.

"Doesn't matter whether he actually screwed them or not. He got off on the murders. That was why he killed them. To him, it was a messed-up act of love. Millhouse didn't love Hilton."

"Then why her? Why didn't he pick someone at random?"

Erin had been wondering that herself. "It would've made it easier to get away with if he'd killed a stranger," she said. "And that was the thing he lied about. So why Annmarie Hilton? Who was she to him?"

"You think they were screwing?"

"You always think this is about sex, don't you."

"You just said that Heartbreak bastard did it for sex. That's what serial killers do! They're messed up in the head and they can't have healthy sex lives. It wouldn't be the first time a good-looking prof got it on with a student."

"Maybe," she said. "But I'm thinking about her studying psychopaths. I think Millhouse took the class for a couple of reasons."

"What, you don't believe he wanted to join the FBI?"

"Not a chance. Their psych screening would've raised all kinds of red flags. Quantico wouldn't touch him with a ten-foot pole. No, he did it for one of two reasons."

"Okay, Professor O'Reilly. Is there gonna be a test on this?"

"The obvious one is that he wanted to know about other psychopaths, so he could avoid their mistakes. He could fine-tune his technique."

"I'll buy that. And the other?"

"Maybe he was genuinely curious about himself," she said. "Teenagers are trying to figure out who they are. It's possible he was just looking for information so he'd understand his own feelings."

"Or lack thereof," Vic said. "But then why whack the professor?"

"Saunders pegged him as a psychopath after one meeting," Erin said. "Hilton would've seen a lot more of him, and she was trained to recognize people like him. I think while he was studying himself, she was studying him. Maybe she found out something he didn't want her to know."

* * *

Back at Major Crimes, they found Webb and Agent Johnson. The Homeland agent was at the office's extra desk, typing up a report on a laptop. Webb was reading something on his computer and fidgeting, clearly getting ready to take a smoke break.

"Welcome back, Detectives," Johnson said. He smiled. "I think we're just about done with this unpleasant little situation."

"What do you need us to do?" Erin asked.

"I'd like you to talk to the roommate, Forster," Johnson said. "Turner claims Forster's an idiot and didn't know anything about what was going on, but I'd like you to grill him just in case. Assuming he's innocent, we'll turn him loose. I've sent you Turner's statement. He spilled everything."

"Did he say anything about Christopher Millhouse?" she asked.

Johnson shook his head. "Nothing about him. I don't think they even knew one another."

"Sometimes there really are coincidences, O'Reilly," Webb said.

"If you say so, sir," she said, unconvinced. "What happens to Turner?"

"Florence Supermax," Vic guessed. "Or maybe Guantanamo Bay."

"No," Johnson said. "He'll be under the aegis of Homeland Security. We'll keep him under close observation, but he works for us now."

"You're using him as a security consultant," Erin said, understanding. "You were already interested in recruiting him. Now you've got leverage so he's got no choice."

"Got it in one, Detective," Johnson said. He was still smiling. "With his talent, Turner could've made a lot more money in the private sector."

"But now that you've got his nuts in a vise, you can make him do whatever you want," Vic said. "Jesus. And you're supposed to be the good guys."

Johnson's smile vanished. "We are the good guys," he said. "You were living in New York when the towers came down, Detective Neshenko. You've seen what the bad guys do. We got lucky last night. A genius prankster exposed a serious security flaw in our power grid. All he did was shut off the lights for a couple of hours. A real terrorist could've done incalculable damage."

"People died," Erin said angrily.

"We're at war," Johnson said. "Wars have casualties. And innocent people pay the price for our mistakes. I understand you don't like it, but what happened is in the past. What we want is to make sure the people who are still alive are protected in the future."

"If bin Laden had offered to work for the TSA, would you have offered him a deal?" Vic demanded.

"Yeah, I would," the agent said. "Then, once I got him in a sealed room, I would've killed him with my bare hands. But Scott Turner isn't Osama bin Laden. He's just a kid who's really bright in some ways and really dumb in others."

"I hate making deals with crooks," Vic muttered.

Erin fell silent. She was thinking about Carlyle and his immunity deal with the District Attorney. He'd done worse than Turner had. Carlyle had laundered money for the Mob, blown up garbage trucks for them, and even killed a man with his own hands. If she could forgive him all that, who was she to throw stones at Agent Johnson, who was just doing his job?

"You guys have been at war so long, I wonder how you'll know when it's over," Vic said.

"That's the trouble," Johnson agreed. "It's a rough deal, no matter how you slice it."

"Now that we can agree on," Vic said.

Erin left Rolf to take an afternoon nap, heading down to fetch Forster. Vic came with her, still grumbling.

"We're not a damn recruitment agency for the Feds," he said.

"They'll keep him on a short leash," she said. "Anyway, he's not our problem anymore."

"No, we get to lean on the dumb frat boy. Lucky us."

They found Forster in the holding cell farthest from Millhouse's. A uniform was patrolling Holding, making sure the various teenagers didn't communicate to sync up their stories. The jock was pacing his cell like an unhappy zoo animal. He was pale, his eyes darting frantically around. When he saw Erin and Vic, a mingled look of fear and hope came into his face.

"You guys gonna let me out of here?" he asked, gripping the bars. "I swear, I didn't do anything!"

"We're going to have a little chat," Erin said.

"Face the wall," Vic ordered. "Cross your hands behind your back."

Forster whined, but did as he was told. Vic cuffed him and they marched him to the interrogation room. On the way, they passed Millhouse's cell. Creepy Chris was sitting exactly the way he had the last time Erin had seen him, still humming classical music. He made eye contact with Erin and smiled in a way he'd probably learned from a Stanley Kubrick movie. She resisted the urge to give him the finger and kept walking instead.

"Forty-one hours, Detectives," Millhouse called mockingly after them.

"God, I hate that guy," Vic muttered.

"What's Chris doing here?" Forster asked.

Erin didn't answer until they had him in the interrogation room. The kid was scared, so Erin decided to lean into his fear and see what she could squeeze out of him. She got right in his face, no preliminaries.

"How did you know Turner's plan?" she snarled.

"I didn't... I didn't have anything to do with it!" Forster stammered. "You've gotta believe me! I don't know shit about computers! That's why I was borrowing his! Because mine's such a piece of junk! His can run games with no lag spike at all. I was just doing some deathmatches with the other guys online."

"Answer the question!" Erin snapped. "You knew what he was doing. How?"

She didn't know that for certain, but Forster didn't know she was bluffing. He wilted under her stare.

"He was bragging about it," the kid said miserably. "Said he knew how to hack the city, that he was gonna do it to show he could. He said it'd be epic, that the thing would make the national news."

"He was right about that," she said grimly. Then she made a guess. "How do you know Chris Millhouse?"

"That creep? I hardly know him at all! Whatever he did, I had nothing to do with it!"

"Who said he did anything?" she retorted.

"You've got him locked in a cell," he said, not unreasonably.

"We've got you in a cell," Erin volleyed back. "You saying you did something?"

"No! This is a mistake! Look, my parents are coming down this weekend. You gotta let me out before then! They're gonna kill me!"

"You're worried about your parents? You're looking at hard time as an accessory," she said. "Unless you cooperate. Chris Millhouse. When's the last time you saw him?"

"Just a minute ago! In jail!"

Erin clenched her teeth. "Before that, dumbass."

"At a Sigma Nu party," he said. "Last Friday night."

"He's a member of your frat?"

"No way! We'd never pledge a guy like that!"

"Then what was he doing there?"

"He doesn't exactly look like a sorority babe," Vic said. He was standing by the door, examining the floor and looking bored. When Erin decided to play bad cop, it didn't leave much for him to do.

"I don't know!" Forster said. "I was pretty wasted."

"How old are you?" she asked.

"Nineteen. Almost twenty."

"What were you drinking?"

"I don't know. Whatever was in the bowl. Plus a couple beers. Like I said, I was trashed. But I remember Creepy Chris. He wanted to talk to me about some stuff."

"What stuff?"

Forster shrugged. "I don't know. Stuff!"

Erin fought down the urge to grab the kid by the collar and shake his memory loose. "Did you tell him about Turner's little prank?"

"Uh... maybe. Things get a little fuzzy. He got me another drink and I kind of blacked out. I don't know what happened after that."

"You saying he roofied you?" Vic asked.

"What do you mean?" Forster looked alarmed. "You mean he... like, did something to me?"

"Not like you're thinking," Erin said. "So Chris was talking to you, he brought you a drink, and you blacked out? That's all you remember? That's not good enough."

"Okay, yeah," Forster said frantically. "I think... yeah, I said something about the lights going out. I said it'd happen last night."

"Royal," Erin said, fixing him with her stare. "Are you just telling me what you think I want to hear? I want the truth."

"No, I told him!" Forster said. "I remember, because he smiled like I'd said something funny. Then, when he handed me the drink, as I was drinking it, he said, 'That's right. Lights out.' And that's all."

"And did you tell anyone else about Turner?" she asked. "Anyone at all?"

"No. At least, I don't think so. I might've said something on Friday, after the drink. I don't remember."

* * *

"Harmless," was Vic's assessment. They'd stepped out of the interrogation room to confer. "Stupid, but harmless."

"Not for Annmarie Hilton," Erin said.

"C'mon, if Millhouse was gonna kill her, he'd have found a way to do it with or without that meathead."

"I agree, he's not an accessory," she said. "But he did help that son of a bitch."

"And he didn't report Turner's dumbass plan," Vic added. "Who was it who said the only thing you gotta do for the bad guys to win is nothing?"

"JFK said it, I think," Erin said. "He was quoting somebody else, I think. But he had a point."

Vic looked at the clock on the observation room wall. "Almost quitting time," he said. "What do you want to do with this loser?"

"Process him and kick his ass to the curb," she said. "He's wasting our time."

"And the world's oxygen," Vic added.

"And then we should probably help the Lieutenant with all the paperwork," she said without enthusiasm.

"Can't we run down more leads on Millhouse's thing?" Vic pleaded. He'd take almost any excuse to avoid paperwork.

"Sure. Can you think of any?"

Vic thought for a moment. "No," he said. "We can show he knew about the power outage, but I wouldn't bet on that drunken idiot on the witness stand. And we can show Millhouse knew a missing woman. We need evidence."

"I know."

"And Millhouse is right. If we don't get it in the next day and a half, we have to let him go."

"I know!"

"So what do you want to do?"

Erin rubbed her temples. "I want a stiff drink."

"I hear you," Vic said.

"And I want a fancy dinner, a long, hot bath, a massage, and ten hours of uninterrupted sleep."

"You don't ask for much. You want a pony to go with that?"

"Instead, I'm going to do paperwork over crappy takeout and then play cards with a bunch of murderous thugs."

Vic lowered his voice. "Hanging with the O'Malleys tonight?"

"Yeah."

"Good luck with that."

"Thanks."

"How's it going?" He hardly ever asked about her under-cover assignment.

"I'm still breathing, so I guess it's going okay so far."

He smiled grimly. "Say, did you hear the one about the guy who falls out of an airplane? He pulls out his phone and calls his wife while he's free falling, twenty thousand feet up. He tells her what's happening. 'Oh, my God!' she screams. 'You're going to die!'

"The guy replies, 'Honey, why would you say that? I feel fine. So far, it's going okay.'"

"Thanks for the vote of confidence."

"Hey, it's why I'm here."

Chapter 9

Most people pictured Hell as a fiery pit, where sinners got roasted for what they'd done wrong in life and demons stabbed them with giant toasting forks; a sort of eternal diabolical barbecue. Some preferred to think of it as a cold place, all ice and darkness.

Erin knew, whatever it looked like on the surface, if you drilled down deep enough, Hell was a bureaucracy. It was full of forms, pointless paperwork, authorizations, justifications, and red tape. How could it be anything else?

She'd been filling out arrest forms, typing up statements, and of course handling the ubiquitous, infamous DD-5s, and she'd been doing it for hours. Cops got used to the paperwork after a few years on duty, but they never got to like it. It was like pulling a week-old corpse out of an apartment; a nasty, ugly chore, but it was part of the Job and somebody had to do it.

"I've got an idea," she said, more than two hours after her shift should have ended.

"We can't set fire to our Fives," Vic said without looking up. "I tried that at my first posting. Almost burned down the station house. Got a three-day rip."

"I was just thinking we could make the perps in Holding fill out the forms," she said. "It's not like they've got anything better to do."

"Negative," Webb said. "It'd violate their Eighth Amendment rights. And their Fifth Amendment rights, too, if they filled them out correctly. Which they wouldn't."

"I think that's it for mine," Erin said, standing. "And I have somewhere I need to be." Rolf sprang up, more than ready for his evening walk.

"Don't let the door hit your ass on the way out," Vic said.

"Get here early tomorrow," Webb said. "If we want to get something on Millhouse, we'll need to move fast."

She nodded absently, but she was thinking about the upcoming meeting of the O'Malleys, which was on an even tighter deadline. She had to assume some of them would arrive before Carlyle, which meant she needed to be there to roll out the red carpet. And before that, she had a phone call to make, one she didn't dare make from either Major Crimes or her car.

She drove to the parking garage across the street from the Barley Corner, parked, and unloaded Rolf. They set off around the neighborhood. Walking outdoors was about as secure from eavesdropping as possible. She took out her separate cell phone and called Lieutenant Stachowski, her undercover handler.

He picked up right away, just as he always did. "Are you clean?" he asked.

"Everything's fine, Phil," she said. "I just got the word. Evan and his associates are coming to the Corner tonight. Carlyle and Finnegan are on their way back from Chicago. I expect the rest of the gang will be here, too."

"Thanks for the heads-up," Phil said. "Any reason to suspect trouble?"

"No more than usual. But it's been a while since we had one of these card games. Not since..."

"The Connor incident," he finished for her. "Right. But Evan was pleased with that outcome. As long as he's in your corner, you've got nothing to worry about. Any progress on the ledger?"

"No." Phil was talking about Evan's financial records. Nobody knew where he kept them. Without those, they'd never know for sure whether they had the entire O'Malley organization. They needed to be able to seize all Evan's illegal assets, and they needed to know who was on his payroll. It was highly likely he'd infiltrated the NYPD, possibly the FBI as well, and might have politicians in his pocket. To make a clean takedown, they needed it all. And they didn't have it.

"You need to push a little on this," Phil said. "But carefully. He can't know that's what you're doing. But you're one of them now, Erin. They trust you."

"No they don't," she said.

"As much as they trust anyone," he insisted.

"That much, huh?" She snorted. "I'll keep that in mind."

"We can't guarantee a successful outcome without it," he said.

"You don't need to remind me what's at stake!" she said sharply. "I'm living it!"

"I know, Erin. And I'm sorry. Honestly, I never thought this would go on so long. I'd be a lot happier if we'd already ended this operation."

"We'll see it through," she said. "All the way."

"You have your wire?"

"Yeah." She had a recording device sewn into the underwire of her bra. It was an advantage of being female. Guys didn't have a comparable place they could keep a wire. "I'll get the whole thing."

"Be careful."

"You always say that."

"I always mean it."

"I'd hate to break your winning streak," she said. Phil had never lost an undercover officer on an assignment.

"Call me afterward, if you need to talk," he said.

"Copy that."

* * *

The Barley Corner was busy with the after-dinner crowd. Erin ignored the mass of blue-collar drinkers and caught the eye of the slender, quiet young man standing next to the wall. He drifted her direction, limping slightly but still moving with calm efficiency.

"Evening, Ian," she said.

"Evening, ma'am—Erin," Ian Thompson said, catching himself a moment too late. They'd been on a first-name basis for a while now, but Marine Corps habits died hard. "Something up?"

"You hear about the meet tonight?"

"Affirmative," he said. "Mr. Carlyle called me. I've got three guys walking perimeter and another on the cameras. Mason is second-in-command in case something happens to me."

"Nothing's going to happen," she said, hoping it was true. "This is just a meeting."

"Every battle's a meeting until the shooting starts," he said.

"How's the leg?"

"Can't complain." Ian's leg had been badly broken in a gunfight with Mickey Connor and his goons back in June. It was obviously still bothering him, but just as obvious he'd sooner take another bullet than admit it. "Mr. Carlyle said he should be here between 2000 and 2100 hours."

"That's what I heard, too. Any of the gang here yet?"

"Not yet. When they show up, you want them in the back room?"

"Yeah. Thanks."

Ian resumed his position, one carefully chosen to maximize his sight lines in the room. Erin was glad he was there, but wished he'd gone to Chicago with Carlyle. If he had, maybe she wouldn't have been so worried.

She took Rolf upstairs, fed him, and refilled his water bowl. "You're staying here, kiddo," she told him.

Rolf had trouble reproaching her while he was eating, but still managed to give her a soulful look over the lip of his food bowl as he morosely munched his kibble. She retreated downstairs, feeling the pressure of that stare on the back of her neck.

In the main room, she flagged down Caitlin Tierney, Carlyle's most reliable waitress. She explained the special event they were hosting, and that Caitlin's normal duties would be suspended for the evening while she waited on the card game. The woman nodded.

"No problem. I'll be glad to. Mr. O'Malley always gives me a good tip." She giggled. "So does Corky."

"I'll bet he does," Erin said. Caitlin was a young, vivacious, and very pretty redhead; exactly Corky's type. They'd paired up a few times, but it had never turned into anything lasting.

With security and refreshments sorted, Erin went to the back room and laid out the poker chips on the green baize table. She found two brand-new decks of cards and set them next to the chips, leaving the wrappers on. It wasn't that anyone would suspect her of using marked cards or a rigged deck, but it was better to avoid even the appearance.

Then she waited, resisting the urge to check the clock on the wall every ninety seconds. While she waited, she thought.

For all the months she'd worked on infiltrating the O'Malleys, she still knew very little about Evan. Carlyle had told her what he knew, but that hadn't helped much. The O'Malley chieftain was a quiet, private man. He might have his ledger in a safe at his house, or in his apartment, or in a safe-deposit box at any of a dozen banks. It might be hidden away in one of his real-estate holdings, or one of his businesses. It might be electronic, on some dedicated server that wasn't even located in New York State. Maybe he carried it around with him on an electronic tablet. That would be enormously risky, but the sheer audacity of it was an attractive idea.

He had to keep it somewhere he could lay his hands on it whenever he wanted, Erin thought. That ruled out stashing it at a remote location. This was a record that got constantly updated and referenced. If she was head of a Mob family, Erin thought, what would she do?

She'd have it nearby, but in code, she thought. Maybe looking like something else, so nobody would recognize it. But Carlyle or Corky would've seen it after all these years. Evan was careful, but nobody was *that* careful. He must have slipped sometime.

The doorknob started to turn. Erin squeezed the recorder under her blouse, starting the wire running. The door opened and she fought the urge to reach for her gun. She'd left her Glock upstairs, since this was a friendly meeting, but her backup revolver was in its ankle holster just in case.

The first man through the door was a reassuring one, though his face was alarming. Lawrence Mason was a Marine who'd served with Ian in Iraq and brought back a souvenir from the desert in the form of puckered scars on both cheeks. An insurgent's bullet had gone straight in one cheek and out the other, taking several of Mason's teeth with it. Reconstructive surgery had done what it could, but Mason still carried the look of a dangerous man not to be trifled with.

"Ma'am," Mason said. He stepped aside and an even more alarming figure entered the room.

Gordon Pritchard, better known as "Snake," was Evan O'Malley's number-one muscle guy, promoted to replace the late, unlamented Mickey Connor. Erin's eyes went to the man's terrible facial scars, but she forced herself not to stare. Pritchard wasn't a big man, but he radiated cold, venomous purpose. He was the sort of man Erin never wanted standing behind her.

Pritchard nodded to her. "Evening," he rasped. His throat had been badly burned by the firebomb that had broiled the right half of his body, leaving him with a harsh, ugly voice.

"Nice of you to drop by," Erin said. "Everything going well?"

Pritchard shrugged. "Business. You?"

"The same. Have a seat."

Pritchard took it as a suggestion rather than a request. He moved so his back was to the wall and he faced the door, remaining on his feet. Erin knew he was armed. She reminded herself he wasn't there to attack her. She wished she knew more about him. Like Corky and Carlyle, he was former IRA. His police jacket told her he'd done time for aggravated assault. But that was it. He had no family, no personal connections. He was Evan's loaded gun, to be pointed at the O'Malleys' enemies.

It was uncomfortable sharing the room with Pritchard, but fortunately, Evan himself arrived only a couple of minutes later. Mousy, quiet little Maggie Callahan trailed behind him. The O'Malley chieftain offered Erin his hand.

"Good evening, Miss O'Reilly," he said. "I hope I'm finding you well."

"I'm good, thanks," she said. "Sit down, please. Carlyle should be here any minute. He's on the way from the airport with Finnegan."

"So I understand," Evan said. He politely helped Maggie with her coat. The woman sat in the dealer's chair, unwrapped one of the fresh decks of cards, and started shuffling.

Maggie never played cards with the others. She just dealt. Erin wondered, not for the first time, what Maggie did for the O'Malleys. She had no criminal record whatsoever. Her file with the NYPD existed purely because she was a known associate of Evan O'Malley, and consisted of a single sheet of paper attesting to that fact. They wouldn't even have that if not for Erin's investigation. She'd never been arrested, nor even fingerprinted. And she was no gangster. Erin had been hanging out with mobsters for a long time now and Maggie didn't fit the mold.

In Erin's experience, Mob guys fell into one of three categories: soldiers, earners, and bosses. Soldiers were violent thugs who were willing to hurt or kill other people for money. It was a job that required a particular mindset, but no great intelligence or skill. They were dangerous and ultimately replaceable. Mickey Connor had been an exceptional soldier, but still just a thug. Earners were more important. They were the ones who actually committed the crimes that kept organized crime solvent. Earners might do just about anything: gambling, racketeering, burglaries, armed robberies, hijackings, grand theft auto, counterfeiting, and dozens of other crimes. The possibilities were endless. If it made money, they'd do it. The bosses ran the business and made sure the money kept flowing to the right places.

Pritchard was a soldier. Evan was a boss. Carlyle was an earner who'd become a boss. But Maggie? She wasn't any of the three. Maybe she was involved in some sort of quiet illegal activity, securities fraud or something. Evan had never said what she did. Neither had Carlyle, which meant he didn't know. And that was concerning.

While Erin was mulling this over, the door swung open again, admitting James Corcoran and Veronica Blackburn. Veronica had an arm wrapped around Corky's waist and was pressed up close against him, letting him feel that her body was warm, female, and right there. Her face was heavily made up, disguising the lines of age and hard usage, and she was dressed as provocatively as usual. She was looking at Corky with bedroom eyes. Corky was smiling, but the smile was brittle and Erin thought he looked awfully uncomfortable.

"Evening, all," Corky said, taking his attention away from Veronica with almost palpable relief and extricating himself from her clutch. "Who's a lad got to shag to get himself a drink?"

"I'm sure something could be arranged," Veronica purred.

Caitlin poked her head into the room. "Get you anything, ladies and gents?" she asked brightly.

"House whiskey," Erin said. "Neat."

"I'll have sex on the beach, dear," Veronica said.

"Glen D, double shot," Corky said. "Straight up, love."

"Guinness," Pritchard said. "Bring the bottle."

"I'll have what Miss O'Reilly's having," Evan said. "And a mineral water for Maggie."

Since they were still waiting on Carlyle and Finnegan, there was an awkward pause while Caitlin fetched their drinks. Pritchard stayed standing.

"How do you like New York?" Erin asked him.

"Beats Jersey," Pritchard said.

"Tell us something we don't know, lad," Corky said.

"Beats Belfast, too."

"Now those are fighting words," Corky said. "Belfast's the finest city ever raised out of a peat bog."

"If it's so fine, what are so many Irishmen doing over here?" Pritchard retorted.

"On account of the bloody English," Corky said. "I'll be the first to admit, there's more opportunities this side of the pond. But there's no finer place to be from."

"I wouldn't know," Erin said. "I was born in Queens. How about you, Veronica?"

"Hell's Kitchen," Veronica said. "Before it forgot where it came from."

"Mr. O'Malley?" Erin prompted. "You've got a Notre Dame ring. Are you from Indiana?"

For a moment she thought he wouldn't answer. He just stared at her with those cold blue eyes. They stabbed her like icicles. Then, with a shrug she could hear in his voice, he said, "County Cork, but not for long. I wasn't quite five when I came over with my folks. I grew up in Queens, not too far from you. I went to Notre Dame for my business degree. Tried for Harvard, but didn't have the pedigree."

"If you'd got in there, we'd not be sitting here talking about it," Corky said. "You'd be sipping cocktails in Midtown with the other Ivy League bastards, networking with the best of them."

"Probably," Evan said evenly. "It would have advantages."

"Aye," Corky said cheerfully. "When those Wall Street lads get caught with their hands in the biscuit tin, the government comes to their rescue. When we get nicked, we get hauled upstate."

"Maggie?" Erin said.

Maggie's hands slipped. She fumbled the deck of cards, spilling them across the table. "What?" she asked, seeming very startled to have been directly addressed.

"Where did you go to school?"

"Notre Dame," Maggie said, darting a quick glance Evan's direction. That glance told Erin volumes. Evan had smoothed the way for her, had gotten her in and probably paid most or all of her tuition.

"What did you study?"

"Mathematics. Probability and statistics."

"How did you get acquainted with this crew?" Erin asked, cocking her head at the assembled gangsters.

"This is all very touching," Evan said quietly. "But we're not a support group. We're not swapping life stories. It's not a very interesting topic of conversation."

Maggie looked back down at the cards. A slight tremor ran through her. Erin could see the woman's lips moving and thought she heard a very soft muttering that sounded like chains of numbers.

"Sorry," Erin said. "Just making conversation." She'd overstepped. She hoped, not too badly.

"How about the Yankees?" Corky volunteered. "Now there's a cheerful topic."

"Not particularly," Pritchard growled. "Unless you find funerals happy."

"Worst they've done in over twenty years," Corky agreed. "On the bright side, they've nowhere to go but up."

That set the table talking about the Yankees' prospects for the following season. Erin mentally thanked Corky for the save. Whatever Maggie had been about to say, Evan had been quick to put the kibosh on it. If Evan wanted Maggie's past kept secret, it was something Erin very much wanted to know. The question was how to go about finding it out without tipping Evan off.

Caitlin returned with a tray. Erin was glad to see Carlyle right on her heels, neatly dressed as ever. With them was Kyle Finnegan, looking as if he'd slept in his clothes and hadn't bothered to comb his hair.

"Attend the lords of France and Burgundy, Gloucester," Finnegan said by way of greeting.

Erin had learned to take Finnegan's odd outbursts in stride. He was a little weird, his brains having been scrambled by crooked union reps a few years earlier. Those were the guys he was believed to have bludgeoned to death with the very same tire iron they'd used to crack his skull.

"Glad you could join us, gentlemen," Evan said. "How was your trip?"

"We shall express our darker purpose," Finnegan went on. "Give me the map there. Know that we have divided in three our kingdom; and 'tis our fast intent to shake all cares and business from our age, conferring them on younger strengths while we unburdened crawl toward death."

"Everything went to plan," Carlyle translated. "The Chicago lads understand the new arrangement with the Lucarellis. It ought to be a smooth transition."

"Excellent," Evan said. "Now that we're all here, we can start. Maggie?"

Maggie passed out the chips with deft, practiced movements. She dealt the first hand of Texas hold 'em and the game began.

Chapter 10

Erin reflected, as she considered the game, that she had a pretty good group in front of her if she wanted to learn about psychopaths. Evan was the classic type, without a shred of empathy or compassion. He studied people the way one would study a mathematical problem, fitting them into his personal ledger as either assets or liabilities. Pritchard was a technician, a professional killer. Finnegan was utterly insane and unpredictable, subscribing to no human law or morality. Veronica was a manipulator, using her body and that of others for her own pleasure or advancement.

Carlyle and Corky were different. She'd once thought Corky might be a psychopath, but now she knew better. He was cocky and reckless to the point of a borderline death wish, but he felt things the same way Erin herself did. And Carlyle was in the wrong room altogether. He'd stumbled into the O'Malleys by accident, at the lowest point in his life. Evan had seen his potential, simultaneously gaining a powerful piece of leverage over him, and he'd been stuck here ever since. Carlyle was a dangerous man, capable of terrible things, but Erin also knew the weight of guilt he carried.

And then there was Maggie. Erin resisted the urge to stare at the woman. What was she to Evan? Mistress? That didn't scan. Evan had never shown any inclination toward promiscuity, and his behavior toward Maggie might be polite and a little overprotective, but never affectionate. Maggie herself was one of the least sexy, or even sexual, people Erin had ever seen. Just having her in the same room with a sexpot like Veronica was an oxymoron.

"A hundred fifty to you, darling," Carlyle said quietly, reminding her there was a game of poker happening.

"Call," Erin said absently, adding her chips to the pot. She was only paying the slightest attention to her cards. Fortunately, she was gambling with Carlyle's money.

Could Maggie be Evan's illegitimate daughter? Now there was a thought. But again, Evan showed no indication of personal fondness toward her. He treated her more like a valued employee than a member of his family. But if that was the case, what did Maggie do? If the other woman was a chemist, Erin might have suspected her of concocting drug cocktails. But Maggie had said she'd studied math and had sounded like she was telling the truth. Erin had the idea Maggie would be an absolutely terrible liar.

"Three jacks," Corky said proudly, laying down his cards. "I'd love to see the hand can top this one."

Nobody could make a better showing, so he raked in his winnings. "It's my lucky night," he said, winking at Caitlin, who was standing by to freshen the players' drinks. She smiled and puckered her lips, blowing him an air kiss.

Veronica pouted and slid a hand under the table. Corky started as if he'd been stung. Erin wondered just what Veronica had done to him. The madam was really putting the moves on him tonight. Corky smiled almost as brightly as usual, but he was definitely uncomfortable with the situation.

What use would Evan have for a mathematically-inclined, socially-awkward, isolated young woman? The O'Malleys were big into gambling. Maybe Maggie was an expert at odds-making. Maybe she was like Dustin Hoffman in *Rain Man*, some sort of hidden genius with numbers.

Erin tried to think of a way to test her theory. Ideally, she'd want to do it when Evan wasn't around. She settled in to wait for her opportunity and focused her attention on her cards as best she could. That was a good idea anyway. With Corky's luck running the way it looked to be, she'd have to be careful if she wanted to hold onto some chips.

Corky continued his hot streak, interrupted only when Finnegan embarked on an apparently deranged bout of one-upmanship in the betting. Corky assumed Finnegan was bluffing, and doing it badly and obviously, until Finnegan revealed an ace and a six, which matched the pair of aces and six on the table to make a full house.

"Bloody hell," Corky muttered as Finnegan blinked and collected the biggest pot of the night with an air of distracted inattention. "That scunner's better at this than he lets on. He's a bloody hustler. Hiding in plain sight, he is."

Corky's last sentence echoed in Erin's mind. *Hiding in plain sight*, she thought. She remembered a case from last year in which she'd gone up against a master of misdirection only to learn that there'd been no trick at all. Everything had been exactly what it appeared to be, and the very obviousness had nearly let a man get away with murder.

Why was she thinking of that now? Was it Millhouse's smug confession? The question of Maggie's role in the O'Malleys? Evan's elusive ledgers?

She couldn't think. Erin decided to lubricate her brain a little more and see if that helped. She signaled Caitlin.

"Another Glen D," she said. "Straight up."

"Make that two," Carlyle said.

"Three," Corky chimed in. "No, four, come to that. You can bring me two glasses, or just pour it into one. It'll all end in the same place."

"On the way," Caitlin said with a brilliant smile. She flounced out of the room, Corky thoughtfully considering her rear end as she left.

Evan stood. "I'll be right back," he said. Pritchard likewise rose and accompanied his boss out of the room.

"I've heard of lasses going to the washroom in pairs," Corky commented once the door had closed. "But not typically the lads."

"It depends on which lads," Carlyle said. "A bodyguard's no bad thing to have about you."

"If I can't guard my own body, it's not worth protecting," Corky scoffed.

"I'll guard your body," Veronica purred. She shifted her chair closer to his and laid a hand on his thigh. "What do you think, Corky? I can guard you very, very closely. Night and day."

"I'm not on the market just now," Corky said. "But if I'm in need, you'll be the first to know."

Erin took advantage of the moment to lean in toward Maggie. "Can I ask you something?" she said.

Maggie blinked at her. Erin took that as a yes.

"What're my chances of pulling an inside straight?" she asked.

"Depends on what's already been played," Maggie said quietly, looking down at the cards and expertly shuffling them. "One in thirteen, roughly."

"You're pretty good with numbers," Erin said. "I always had trouble with math. Could never remember all the formulas."

Maggie seemed confused. "Why not?"

"So many numbers," Erin said. "Don't you ever forget numbers?"

"No."

"What do you mean?"

"I don't forget them," Maggie said. "Never. I've got them all. Up here." She tapped the side of her head with her forefinger.

"Total recall, huh? That's amazing."

Maggie shrugged slightly and returned her attention to the cards. Erin was suddenly aware of eyes on her. She looked across the table into Finnegan's watery, distant gaze.

"No man has a good enough memory to be a successful liar," Finnegan said.

"I've heard that before," Carlyle said. "What lad first said it?"

"A politician," Finnegan said.

"Well, they'd certainly understand the business of lying," Carlyle said.

"He was important a hundred and fifty years ago, or thereabouts," Finnegan said. "I doubt you've heard of him. Abraham something-or-other."

"Lincoln?" Erin guessed.

Finnegan snapped his fingers. "That's it! How did you know? I can't believe you know him too."

Erin gave Carlyle a brief, helpless look. He raised an eyebrow and shook his head. There was no accounting for Kyle Finnegan.

Evan and Pritchard returned, which was just as well. Erin didn't dare press Maggie any further in the presence of others. But the inkling of an idea had struck her. She really wanted to discuss it with Carlyle. From that moment, she was just eager for the game to end so they could get rid of all these gangsters and have a serious conversation.

That was the trouble of organized crime. It was a lot easier to get into than out of. Erin was stuck in this card game with these criminals until Evan called a halt. So she drank her whiskey and played the cards that were dealt to her as well as she could. She won a little and lost a lot, and in the end was left with a hundred twenty dollars out of the thousand she'd started with.

Corky had an impressive pile in front of him, but so did Finnegan. Carlyle's usual skill with the cards hadn't helped him much tonight. He and Veronica were flat broke. Pritchard had also lost heavily. Evan had broken even, as he always seemed to do. It was a little uncanny, suggesting he was choosing not to win.

"I think we'll call it a night," Evan said, standing up. "Thank you all for coming. And everyone please remember not to make waves with the Oil Man's crew. We're supposed to be at peace, so I don't want to hear about anyone mixing it up with any Italians."

"How about Sicilians?" Corky asked.

"That's the same thing," Carlyle said.

"Not to them it isn't," Corky said. "Just ask a Sicilian. He'll likely stab you for suggesting it. Great stabbers, those Sicilian lads. Always carrying knives on them."

"Where are we going next, Corky?" Veronica asked, nestling close to him. "I have a few suggestions."

"I'm sure you do," Carlyle said. "But I fear I'm needing Mr. Corcoran's services as well, in a matter of business."

"The stern call of duty," Corky said with false regret, disentangling himself from her. "I'll bid you a fond goodnight."

Veronica's puffed lips, bright scarlet, made an exaggerated pout. "Are you sure?" she asked. She lowered her voice slightly. "He can't do the things I can for you."

"And I'm glad of it," Corky said. "There's some things a lad's best mate shouldn't have to venture on his behalf. Good night, Vicky."

Veronica reluctantly trailed out after Evan, Pritchard, Maggie, and Finnegan, leaving just Erin, Corky, Carlyle, and Caitlin.

"We'll not be needing you further, Caitlin," Carlyle said.

"Speak for yourself, Cars," Corky protested. "I know you're practically married these days, but I'll not have you running all the colleens out of my neighborhood!"

"It's all right, lass," Carlyle said with a smile. "I promise I'll not keep him long. If you'd shut the door behind you?"

Caitlin gave Corky a last smile and did as she was told.

Corky turned to Carlyle. "Not that I'm ungrateful for the rescue," he said, "getting me out of Vicky's claws. But what's up?"

"Erin has something to share with us," Carlyle said.

Erin was startled. "How did you know?"

Carlyle's smile crinkled the corners of his eyes. "I know you, darling. You thought of something in the middle of the game. It was troubling you the whole time. Your play improved a bit once you'd come to your conclusion, but not enough to save you. You were scarcely thinking of the cards. A bit disrespectful of the money I staked you."

"Was I that obvious?" she asked, dismayed. "Do you think Evan noticed?"

"He surely noticed your mind wasn't on the game," Carlyle said. "But he'd not know why. Fortunately, there's many a thing can cross the mind of a copper, and most of them have naught to do with Mr. O'Malley's interests."

"Well, this one does," she said. "And thanks for keeping Corky around. I think we might need him."

"I'm at your service, love," Corky said. "I'll lay down my body for you. I mean it. Anytime, anywhere. Right here on the card table, if that's what you're wanting."

"I don't need that kind of service," Erin said with a smile. "But if you really want to help, you can work your charms on someone else."

He blinked. "Erin, love, you never cease to amaze. Who's the lucky lass?"

"Maggie Callahan."

There were ten seconds of dead silence. Then Corky, no trace of his usual smile, broke it.

"You'd best explain yourself," he said softly.

"She's the key," Erin said.

"To what?" Corky asked.

"To everything. She's Evan's accountant."

"How do you figure?"

"Evan doesn't keep books," she said, looking at Carlyle for confirmation. "At least, not physical ones anyone's ever seen. You'd know, wouldn't you?"

Carlyle nodded slowly. "Aye, but his accounts are too complicated to keep in one's head."

"In my head, sure," Erin said. "Or yours, or especially Corky's."

"No call for that, love," Corky said indignantly.

"But what about Maggie's?" Erin went on. "She claims her memory is—"

"Perfect," Carlyle finished in unison with her.

"Nobody's got a memory that good," Corky said. "Not good enough for a lad like Evan to trust his business to. And he'd be mad to trust his accounts to one brain. Suppose she ran off? Or died?"

"I expect he'd keep a backup," Carlyle said thoughtfully. "In case of mischance. And he'd have to update it every so often. But

Maggie's head for numbers might just be good enough for his everyday affairs, so he'd not have to carry his ledgers about him. Nay, that just might work. It's rather brilliant, now you mention it."

"We don't need Evan's books," Erin said. "We just need Maggie."

"You say that like it's easy," Carlyle said. "He keeps her close about him. Uncommonly close. I wonder I'd never given much thought to it."

"You're the same way," she said. "With Ian. And before that, in Ireland... with Siobhan," she finished quietly. Carlyle's surrogate daughter was still something of a sore subject, even months after her death.

"Aye," Carlyle said. "Bit of a blind spot for me. Are you sure, darling?"

"How can I be sure?" she replied. "But it's the only thing I can think of. When Evan's talking to his business associates, making deals, is Maggie there?"

"Aye," Carlyle said again. He was nodding now. "Whenever he's discussing that side of the business, she's always nearby. Never says much."

"You mean she never says anything," Corky said. "Quiet as a churchmouse, the lass is. Half the time, you forget she's sitting there."

"Which is precisely the point," Carlyle said. "Come to that, Erin, it scarcely matters if you're right or not. With her head for figures, and her access, I'd wager she remembers most of what we're needing, regardless of whether it's her job or not."

"We just need to get her to say what she knows," Erin said. "On a wire. Then we've got Evan by the balls."

"That simple, aye?" Corky asked.

"That's where you come in," Erin said.

"Me?" He raised his eyebrows. "What the devil am I supposed to do about that?"

"Win her over," Erin said. "Charm her. Find out what she knows. Get her to spill."

"That's your plan?" Corky said. To Erin's astonishment, he sounded genuinely angry; a side of him she'd rarely seen. "I'm to seduce her and get the goods? Toy with her heart?"

"That's the idea, yeah," Erin said.

"No."

The word was flat, hard, and heavy, leaving no room for discussion. Carlyle, knowing Corky better than Erin did, reached for her hand to pull her aside. But Erin tugged free and tried again.

"Why not?" she demanded. "It's not like you don't know how."

"I'm no one's bloody whore!" Corky exploded. "I like the lasses, sure enough, I've made no bloody secret of that, but I'll not be a party to using people that way! Forget about me, and whatever blooming self-respect I've still got. Think about Maggie. She's harmless. She's practically a civilian. I'll not be betraying her; not for you, Erin, nor you, Cars, nor even for God Himself if He was to ask. Am I making myself clear?"

"Okay," Erin said. "I get it. But—"

"It's not a question of bloody necessity," Corky went on. He scooped up a glass from the table, which happened to be Erin's. He made an angry gesture with it, then realized it still held half a shot of Carlyle's good top-shelf whiskey. The amber liquid sloshed back and forth. He paused, stared at it a moment, opened his mouth, and tossed it back at one gulp.

"It's all right, lad," Carlyle said. "She didn't mean anything by it."

"It's cruel," Corky said in a softer tone. "I'll kill a lad if he crosses me, but I'll never make a lass suffer. The world's hard enough." Then, almost as an afterthought, he threw the shot glass across the room. It hit the wall and exploded in a glittering shower of shards. While Erin and Carlyle were watching the glass's final flight, Corky spun on his heel, yanked open the door, and was gone.

"Shit," Erin said quietly.

"It's all right," Carlyle repeated. "I'll talk to him. Best to let the lad go for now. He'll cool down."

"I never thought he'd react that way," she said. "I just thought... God, Maggie's a woman and Corky's... well, Corky! He flirts with everybody! If it's female and has a pulse, he's interested."

"But never as a means to an end," Carlyle said. "For Corky it's all about the connection. He'll never pretend to be someone he's not, nor lie his way into a woman's arms. I'm the first to admit, the lad's notions of honor are curious, but he'll stick to his code."

Erin nodded. She leaned against the card table and sighed. "So what do we do?"

"We'll think of something," he said.

Chapter 11

Carlyle went out to the Barley Corner's main room to conduct his usual business, leaving Erin to her own devices. It was a little after eleven, past bedtime for the nine-to-five set, but not even fashionably late by police standards. She went upstairs, where Rolf greeted her with a wagging tail and full forgiveness for having abandoned him. Dogs didn't hold grudges.

The first thing she did was upload the recording of the card game to the secure drop-box Phil had set up. Then she got a Guinness out of the fridge and sat down on the couch. Rolf settled in next to her and prepared for some serious napping.

Erin's thoughts ricocheted back and forth between Maggie Callahan and Chris Millhouse. Maggie seemed innocent but had a secret. Creepy Chris claimed he was a criminal but was confident they couldn't prove it. In both cases, she needed evidence. She didn't care if Maggie got locked up or not; she completely agreed with Carlyle that the woman was harmless on her own. But the more Erin thought about it, the surer she was that Maggie was the key to Evan's operations. She was his Achilles Heel, his Death Star exhaust port, his soft underbelly, his...

Analogies weren't Erin's strong suit. But every opponent, however dangerous, had a weak point. Just as Evan had his, so did Millhouse. She just had to find it.

Erin took another gulp of Guinness. She had a slight buzz going from the whiskey she'd drunk during the game, but she was still thinking clearly. She called Columbia University's Security office, fortunately avoiding Chief Oglesby, and got Annmarie Hilton's emergency contact information. It was still early enough to call California, and a good time to try on a weeknight. The number was for Annmarie's brother Damien, with his address in Santa Monica. She dialed and hoped.

On the third ring, a harried-sounding man picked up. In the background, Erin heard a baby crying.

"Hello?" he said.

"Mr. Hilton?" Erin said. "I'm with the NYPD. My name is Detective O'Reilly. Are you Annmarie Hilton's brother?"

"What? Just a second, ma'am." The man took his mouth away from the phone and said, "Cindy, can you please take him for a moment?"

After a few seconds, he was back on the line. The screaming was still audible, but further away. "Sorry, ma'am," he said. "Yes, this is Damien Hilton. How can I help you?"

"I need to know when you had your most recent contact with Annmarie," Erin said.

"I talked to her, oh, three or four days ago," Damien said. "What's this about? Is she okay?"

Erin closed her eyes. She hated this part of the Job. "That's what we're trying to determine," she said. "Can you think of anywhere she would go if she wasn't at her apartment?"

"She's working at Columbia this term," he said. "In New York. But I guess you'd know that, wouldn't you? Have you talked to the University?"

"Yes, they're the ones who gave me your number."

"Oh."

"Does she have a boyfriend? Any close friends out here?"

"Not that I know of. Ma'am, what's happened to her? Is she missing?"

"Not technically," Erin said, and that was true. Nobody had reported Annmarie missing. The scary thing was, a single adult in a big city could disappear for a surprisingly long time before the police were notified, if they ever were. Erin had experienced her share of Patrol calls in answer to a bad smell in an apartment, only to discover the resident had died several days before, usually of a heart attack, and nobody had known or cared.

"What should we do?" Damien asked. "I mean, we're in California. We've got a three-month-old. We can't really travel. Is there somebody we should call, or what?"

"Let me give you my number," Erin said. "If you hear from her, or from anybody who claims to know anything about her, please find out what you can from them and call me right away. Can you do that?"

"Of course." Damien sounded dazed. One moment his biggest worry had been how to stop his baby crying, the next he was trying to deal with a family crisis.

"We'll let you know as soon as we know anything," Erin assured him. "It may be a couple of days. Try not to worry in the meantime. This may be just a misunderstanding."

It felt like a cheap, useless reassurance, especially since she was pretty sure it wasn't true. She thought Annmarie was dead. But telling the woman's brother her fears wouldn't do anyone any good, and it was possible she was wrong. So she gave him a few more bland platitudes and hung up, trying not to think about the last missing person she'd been trying to track down. That had been her own sister-in-law. It had come out okay in the end, but it had been a very close shave.

Then, mainly because she was still holding the phone, wasn't ready for bed, and didn't know what else to do, she called her dad. It beat sitting alone, drinking and thinking.

This was a little iffy, since Sean O'Reilly was retired and it really was a bit late, but Erin did it anyway. She hoped he wouldn't be mad.

To her relief, he picked up after just two rings. "O'Reilly," he said.

"Hey, Dad," she said. "Everything's okay. I'm glad I didn't wake you up."

"Just down in the den, watching the Yanks at Tropicana in Tampa Bay," Sean said. "Tied at zero going into the Ninth. But I've got to tell you, it ain't looking good. They've given up on the season, and good riddance. What's up?"

"I just wanted to pick your brain a little," she said.

"Pick away, kiddo. It can't hurt any more than watching all those dollars they paid for our starting lineup get pissed away. They can't string more than two hits together in an inning. It's pathetic."

"Did you ever get any unsolicited confessions on the Job?" she asked.

"Sure," he said. "All the time. Nutjobs looking for attention, mostly. Or guys who'd done something stupid and couldn't live with themselves. Had one guy who'd gotten drunk and beat his wife to death because she wouldn't turn off her soap opera and do the dishes. He couldn't believe he'd done it. The bastard wouldn't stop crying."

"I'm not talking about remorse," Erin said. "And it's not some attention whore, either. This guy is different, Dad. I think he did it, but we can't prove it."

Sean cleared his throat. "You've got a murder, and a suspect who claims he did it," he said. "It shouldn't be too hard to tie him to it."

"That's just the thing," she said. "We don't have a murder. Not yet."

"I don't understand. Did he tell you he was going to kill someone?"

"No, he claims he killed her, but we don't have a body, or any hard evidence. Just his word, and that's not enough to hold up in court."

"Who'd he kill? According to him?"

"His psych professor. He said he offed a stranger, but the prof is missing. Didn't turn up for class, won't answer her phone, and isn't at home. Family haven't heard from her either."

"That's suspicious," Sean agreed. "Now, I never made detective, but it sounds circumstantial."

"Yeah. We can't convict without evidence. We can't even charge."

"Why did he confess?"

"He's showing off," she said. "He thinks he's gotten away with it and he wants us to know it."

"Then he's a cocky son of a bitch," he said. "That's how you trip him up."

"Yeah," she said. "But he won't tell us anything we can use. He's too smart. He's just sitting in his holding cell, marking time until his forty-eight hours are up."

"Did he lawyer up?"

"No. He doesn't think he needs one."

"You can always try leaning on him," Sean said thoughtfully. "But it sounds like you need the body."

"Yeah," she said. "Only problem is, we don't know where it is. We know where he says he killed her, but he might be lying."

"How detailed was the confession?"

"He told us what weapon he used, how she looked, how it felt," she said. "It sounded genuine to me. And I think that was the point. Lots of crooks feel the need to tell somebody what they did. So he told us. But he left out what he did with the body."

"What was the scene?" Sean asked. "I assume you walked it?"

"Of course. With Rolf in search mode. He should've smelled out anything there, even if it was just blood. Except..."

"What?" Sean's ears had been tuned for that word.

"Except Rolf started sneezing," she said quietly. "At the scene. Like he had some sort of chemical up his nose."

"What did the area look like?"

"Construction site. Our guy said he brained his victim with a piece of rebar."

"There must be all sorts of chemical stuff lying around that kind of place," Sean said. "You know better than I do what can screw up a dog's nose."

Erin did. "Pepper can do it temporarily," she said. "But only until the dog clears the area. And bleach works okay."

"Did you see any bleach on scene?"

"No." Then Erin clutched the phone, her heart jumping with excitement. "But we found a big bottle of it in our suspect's room."

"Okay, so that's how he spoofed your K-9," Sean said. "And disinfected the scene. But he still had to put the body somewhere. Did he have transportation?"

"He doesn't have a car," Erin said. "He might've borrowed one from one of his frat buddies, I guess. But no. The power was out when it happened."

"I heard about that," Sean said. "It was all over the news."

"He couldn't have gotten far in a car," Erin said. "And I don't think he'd have risked it."

"If he didn't have the ability to move the body..." Sean said.

"...it must still be there," she finished for him. "And that's what he told us. But we didn't see it."

"You said it's a construction site," he said. "Maybe he stashed the body somewhere, like they did with Jimmy Hoffa under Giant Stadium. Just make a frame, mix some cement, and pour it over the body. No muss, no fuss."

"Nobody ever found Hoffa's body," she said. "Not even once they tore down the stadium. There's no proof he was there."

"I know that," Sean said. "But it makes a good story, doesn't it?"

"Yeah," she said, thinking she'd have to ask Corky about Hoffa's death sometime. It wasn't the first time she'd wondered about that. Corky was well connected with the Teamsters and might've heard something conclusive. "You think my guy might've buried the body in cement?"

"Maybe," Sean said. "But if he did, you'll need a court order to dig it up."

She sighed. "I know. But I think I better walk the site again anyway."

"How much time do you have?" he asked. "Before you have to cut your guy loose?"

"Until nine AM, day after tomorrow."

"Then my advice is, sleep on it and go out there in daylight. You'll see things better and you'll be more rested. Oh, no!"

"What?" Erin asked, alarmed by the sudden change in her father's tone.

"It's over," Sean said heavily. "Single by Tampa Bay, knocked in a run. One-nothing. What a crap-out. I guess I'd better get to bed. Hope you have better luck on your end."

"Thanks, Dad. Goodnight."

Erin looked at her phone for a moment, thinking. There was no chance whatsoever of getting to sleep. Her dad was right; if there had been a body at the construction site, it had to still be there. But if it was under concrete, there was very little she could do. Did Millhouse even know how to mix cement? That wasn't exactly the sort of thing a college kid would know how to do. He might've had traces on his clothes or shoes, but Erin was sure he would have gotten rid of the clothing he'd worn. This wasn't a run-of-the-mill idiot who killed out of compulsion. He'd planned this, carefully and meticulously.

"When in doubt, retrace your steps," she said. It was a good way to find something you'd lost, or to pick up clues. If Millhouse had made any mistakes, he would've left a clue somewhere along the way. Where had he been that she knew of?

"Frat party," she told Rolf.

The K-9 raised his head and cocked it. That sounded like they might be going somewhere. He was ready.

"Not you, kiddo," she said. "This one I've got to do by myself. You'd just attract attention."

He settled back with a heavy, heartfelt sigh.

Erin got off the couch and went into the bedroom. She opened the closet and examined her options. Ideally, a twentysomething rookie would be the person to pick for an assignment like this, but she didn't want to take the time to put it through proper channels. As long as she looked as young and sexy as possible, she'd probably get away with it. There'd be hell to pay if campus security found out, but where she was going, nobody would be thinking of calling the cops.

The lighting would probably be low, and most of the witnesses would be drunk. Erin was counting on that. She'd still need a lot of makeup, more than she usually wore. She started pulling clothes out and looking them over. It'd been a long time since she'd been to a frat party. Hopefully things hadn't changed too much since her college days.

Chapter 12

Erin hadn't known for sure whether Sigma Nu would be having a party that night, but she'd thought it was highly likely. CSU had swept Turner's room, but they'd have finished with the scene by now and let the rest of the frat boys back in. The ESU raid on the house must be the talk of the campus. Everybody would be trying to get in and see what was going on. Erin would bet a week's salary there'd be a keg in the kitchen and a bunch of drunk college kids wandering around.

She could hear the music from half a block away. Fighting the urge to pull the hem of her miniskirt down, she concentrated on walking in the highest heels she owned. She'd left her hair loose around her shoulders and was wearing a black tank top with her blouse hanging open over it. No bra and the shortest skirt she could find. The air was cold and she felt half naked. At least the heavy layer of makeup was insulating her face a little.

This was probably a bad idea. Erin hadn't notified campus security. They'd be righteously pissed if they found out. She had no backup. She wasn't even carrying her service sidearm; just her snub-nosed .38 and her Taser, in case she had to deal with any overly friendly frat boys. But Erin needed to know what Millhouse had been doing. She'd done more dangerous undercover jobs. She was conducting a more dangerous operation in her off-hours, for crying out loud. How bad could this be?

She was being stupid. Worse, she was being reckless. Either one of those things could get you killed on the street. But she didn't care. She'd tried and failed to get Vinnie the Oil Man. Too many slick bad guys had already slipped through her fingers. She was damned if she'd let Chris Millhouse weasel out of a murder rap. If that meant taking some chances and getting even further on Chief Oglesby's bad side, that was a price she was willing to pay.

A male undercover might have had trouble getting through the door. But a woman, even one in her mid-thirties, had no problems at all. Erin kept herself in shape, which resulted in several appreciative wolf-whistles and comments. That was part of the plan. If these guys were checking out her body, they weren't looking closely at her face. She made it up the stairs and into the house, only pausing long enough to take the paper cup a random guy pressed into her hand. It was filled with God only knew what, and Erin would no sooner have drunk it than she would've snorted a packet of powder she'd taken off a drug dealer. But having the cup in her hand helped her blend in, so she held on to it.

The house was packed with people who might or might not be legally adults. She drifted through the crowd, reflecting how weird it was that she felt more comfortable at the Barley Corner, among actual criminals and thugs, than here with these overgrown kids.

She'd come here on instinct, remembering Royal Forster's testimony about meeting Millhouse and probably being drugged by him. If she could place Millhouse here, with Rohypnol, she could build one link in the chain that would hopefully hang him out to dry. But how was she going to do that? She couldn't exactly walk up to a sketchy-looking undergrad and ask to buy some date-rape drugs. He'd make her for a cop the moment she opened her mouth.

Erin worked the edges of the party, watching and listening. She saw plenty of underage drinking, lots of lewd behavior, and more than enough things that would get you a citation if you did them on a street corner, but no drug dealing. The music was so loud it felt like it was pounding holes through her skull, and the strobe light some genius had hooked up in the living room was making her eyes water. What was it they said? When the music got too loud, you knew you were too old for the party?

"Hey, baby," a young man said, sliding up alongside her and putting a hand right on her ass. "Some party, huh?"

Erin looked into the flushed face of an intoxicated jock more than a decade younger than she was and reminded herself she was undercover. This wasn't the time to put him in an arm-lock and threaten to break his wrist. She made herself nod in time with the music, hoping he'd be content just to cop a feel and move on.

No such luck. He leaned in close, his breath reeking of cheap booze. "It's a little loud in here," he said. "How about we go upstairs and get acquainted?"

I'm almost old enough to be your mom, Erin thought. *And what would she say if she saw you now?* What she did was start to nod, plastering a goofy grin on her face. Then she twisted her mouth and clutched her stomach. In the process, she spilled her drink all over his shirt.

"Oh, no," she said in a liquid, burbling voice. "I think I'm gonna—"

The jock hastily stepped back, his adolescent libido momentarily curdled by the prospect of imminent vomit.

"Whoa," he said. "Take it easy. Maybe just sit down for a sec. Shit, look at my shirt."

"Bathroom," Erin mumbled.

"Okay, yeah," the kid said. "Through there. Or first door on the right up the stairs."

"Thanks," she gasped, stumbling through the crowd and away from her would-be date. She truthfully wouldn't mind a moment alone to check her makeup and gather her composure.

The downstairs bathroom door was closed, and through it came the sounds of someone actually doing what she'd pretended, so she went upstairs. Her timing was good; a pretty blonde was just leaving as Erin arrived. They exchanged nods and Erin went in, closing and locking the door behind her.

"What are you doing?" she asked her reflection. In the bathroom's cold, unforgiving fluorescent light, nobody would have mistaken her for a sorority girl. She looked tired, worried, and annoyed. This was a waste of time. None of these idiots knew anything. Millhouse was going to walk if she didn't get something on him, and here she was, pissing away the few hours they had before they'd need to turn him loose.

She did take a moment to rearrange her hair and tidy up her mascara. Then she pulled open the bathroom door with a savage yank, stepping out into the upstairs hallway.

She was just in time to see a young man walking into one of the bedrooms with his arm around a girl. In fact, it was the same room ESU had broken into earlier that very day. Erin's Patrol-trained eye caught that the girl was scarcely able to stand; the boy was supporting almost her whole weight. The girl's head lolled on her shoulder. She was either totally trashed on alcohol, or possibly drugged, and Erin didn't think the boy was just planning on tucking her in to sleep it off. And she recognized the boy. It was Royal Forster, fresh out of his holding cell and looking to enjoy his freedom.

Now Erin had to make a quick decision. She was here in an unofficial capacity, without the knowledge or consent of campus security. Arresting this creep again would cause all kinds of hassle, and might actually damage her investigation.

But there was no way Erin O'Reilly was going to walk on past a room where a sexual assault was about to happen, and there was no way this girl was conscious enough to give consent. The door swung shut behind the guy and his victim as Erin quickly approached, slipping a hand into her purse and pulling out her X-26 Taser. She removed the cartridge from the plastic device, leaving a gap at the front of the Taser that she could bridge with an arc of electricity with a pull of the trigger.

The door was closed but wouldn't lock. Campus facilities, or maybe one of the frat boys, had done what they could with duct tape, but the damage Parker's boot had done to the door would take more than that. The lock plate was torn clean out, leaving a several-inch hole.

She eased the door open and closed it behind her as firmly as she could. Forster had the girl down on his bed. He was fumbling at his pants with one hand and groping the semi-conscious girl with the other. The girl was trying to say something, but no coherent words were coming out of her mouth; only a thin trail of saliva.

The fury that boiled up in Erin at the sight was so intense that it startled her. She crossed the room in three quick strides, coming up on Forster just as his jeans hit the floor, pooling around his ankles. He heard her arrival and turned, wearing only a soccer jersey and a comically surprised expression.

On the bed, the girl was saying something that sounded like "No, don't."

That was good enough for Erin. She flicked the trigger on her Taser and brought it in close, catching Forster below the belt. Tasers could be used two different ways; at range or in close quarters. By unloading hers, Erin had rigged her X-26 for close contact. Used this way, it operated like a stun gun, delivering a high-voltage, low-amp shock that temporarily locked up the target's muscles and caused excruciating pain. Erin herself had ridden the lightning when she'd first been issued her Taser. The sensation was unique and very unpleasant, like having a hot oven burner planted inside her muscles. She lacked male anatomy, so could only guess and observe what the jolt did to Forster.

His eyes went very wide. His whole body went rigid. A squeaky, breathy sort of scream escaped him before he folded up at the waist and collapsed in a fetal ball, gasping and choking.

Erin stood over him, watching with an unsympathetic eye. The pain lasted only as long as the electricity was running through his body, but Forster had apparently experienced such an overload of sensation that he was still processing it. He sucked in big, deep breaths and tried to uncurl, but his body wasn't ready to let him.

Erin knelt down beside him and tapped him on the shoulder with the tip of the Taser. "Have I got your attention, Royal?" she asked in calm, conversational tones. She was still shaking with rage on the inside, thinking what would be happening right now if she hadn't been there. What she really wanted, rather than talking to him, was to give him another jolt.

He nodded weakly. Tears were pouring down his cheeks.

"What'd you give her?" Erin asked.

"Don't... know what you're talking... about," he wheezed.

"Don't bullshit me, kiddo," she said. "You only had about a second's worth of juice. Next time I'll let you have the full five. What'd you give her?"

Forster looked up at her with bleary terror. "You can't do that!"

"I just did," Erin growled. "You want to test me on this?" She pulled the trigger on the X-26, holding it close to his face so he could see the arcing blue sparks and hear the distinctive rapid-fire *click-click-click*.

"Jesus!" Forster exclaimed. "I was just having some fun! It didn't mean anything!" He tried to roll over on his ass and scoot away from her, but his back came up against the side of the bed. He was trapped.

"What do you think it'll mean to her?" Erin asked, nodding toward the girl on the bed. The girl's eyes were closed and she appeared to be asleep or unconscious.

"She won't even remember it!" he protested.

"So you did drug her," Erin snarled. "Where'd you get the drugs?"

"Xander Yates!"

"Where's Xander?" She triggered the Taser again, watching the reflection of the sparks in his enormous, streaming eyes. As an interrogation tool, the mere threat of it was proving very effective.

"At the party! Downstairs! In the kitchen!" Forster was babbling, staring at the Taser as if it was a poisonous snake.

"Here's what we're going to do," Erin said grimly. "We're going to go downstairs and you're going to put me in touch with Mr. Yates. And trust me, you do not want to screw with me."

"Okay! Okay! Sure! Whatever!"

"Get up," she said, rising to her own feet. "Now."

Forster scrambled up, then immediately fell down again as his feet tangled in his jeans. He hit the floor with a thump. While he got himself sorted out and pulled up his pants, Erin did a quick check of the girl's vitals. She was breathing shallowly and her pulse rate was low, but not dangerously so.

"Don't," Erin said, pointing at Forster without even bothering to look at him. The kid froze in place. He'd been thinking of running, obviously, but he was now so scared of Erin that he didn't dare disobey. She really should've brought her handcuffs, but she hadn't been anticipating having to arrest anyone.

The girl was drifting in and out of consciousness. Erin gave her shoulder a shake.

"What's your name, kiddo?" she asked. "Talk to me."

"Milly," the girl slurred.

"Stay awake, Milly," Erin said. "We're getting you out of here. Come on. Up we get."

She slung Milly's arm around her neck and got her own left arm around the girl's waist, hoisting her up. Fortunately, Milly was slender and didn't weigh much, so Erin was able to keep her Taser in her right hand. She approached Forster.

"You're going to carry her downstairs," she said. "You're not going to drop her, or bump her into anything. You're going to walk slowly and gently. I'll be right behind you. If you try anything, anything at all, you'll regret it."

Forster was no hardened criminal. The shot to his groin had taken the fight out of him. He obediently picked Milly up, like a bridegroom crossing a threshold, and carried her. Erin, true to her word, stayed close behind him, ready to react if he did anything stupid. He might be a coward, but he was also an idiot, so she kept a close eye on him.

Once they were about halfway down the stairs, Erin was able to see into the living room. She picked out a group of young women who were standing clear of the jocks and looked more or less sober. She gave Forster a nudge. He jumped and almost dropped Milly.

"See those four girls by the window?" she asked.

He nodded.

"We're going over there," she said.

The girls looked them over as they approached. One of them, a tall brunette, stepped forward.

"Milly?" she said.

Milly, in Forster's arms, groaned softly but made no other response.

"What did you do to her?" the brunette demanded. "You little shit!" Eyes suddenly blazing, she took another step, wound up, and let Forster have it with a roundhouse right. He only saw it coming an instant before the impact, thanks to the strobe lights, and with his arms holding Milly's body, he had no chance to block or dodge. If she'd used a closed fist, the blow would have cranked his head clean around, but the girl struck with an open-hand slap. There was a loud, meaty *smack* as she nailed him square on the cheek.

Erin darted forward, knowing what was bound to happen. Forster let go of Milly's upper body and the drugged girl started to tumble toward the floor. Erin got her hands under the falling girl just in time, arresting her momentum less than an inch from the floorboards.

The brunette's hands went to her mouth. "Oh my God!" she gasped. "I'm so sorry! I didn't think—"

"Help me," Erin said, trying to maneuver Milly back upright. The brunette and one of her friends knelt down to assist.

"What's the matter with her?" the friend asked.

"You know her?" Erin asked, looking at the brunette.

"Of course! She's on my floor," the girl said. "We're friends. But who are you?"

Erin reached into her handbag and flashed her shield without taking it all the way out. "I'm with the NYPD," she said quietly. "What's your name, miss?"

"Angie," the brunette said. "Angie Ordway."

"Okay, Angie Ordway," Erin said. "I'm trusting you to get Milly home safe. She should be fine. She hasn't been assaulted or anything. Make sure she understands, nothing happened to her. Okay?"

"But what—" Angie began.

"This dipstick here drugged her," Erin said grimly. Then she realized, belatedly, that the dipstick in question was no longer standing where she'd left him.

Cursing inwardly, Erin stood up and scanned the room. Royal Forster was a tall, athletic guy. She caught a glimpse of him on his way toward the back of the house, trying to make a run for it. But he'd plowed into a circle of guys around the keg and that had slowed him down a little.

"You got this?" Erin said quickly, giving Angie a meaningful look.

Angie bit her lip, looking suddenly about five years younger, but nodded. "Yeah," she said.

"Good." Then Erin was off, threading the crowd as well as she could. She wished for Rolf, who would've ended this chase almost before it began. She wished for Vic, who could plow people out of his way like an offensive lineman. But mostly she wished she was wearing sensible shoes.

She ducked a careless arm that nearly clotheslined her, spun around a pair of dancing kids, lunged through a narrow gap between two frat boys, put a foot wrong, nearly twisted an ankle in her damn high heels, tumbled headlong, turned her fall into a forward roll, and came up in the kitchen doorway.

She stood up right in the face of a boy who was coming out with a plate of pizza rolls. She caught the plate right in the middle of her forehead. The plate shattered, spewing ceramic shards and cheap snack food in all directions. Erin blinked stupidly, staring into the eyes of a very surprised and now sauce-stained young man.

"Uh... are you okay?" he asked, almost as dazed as she was by the sudden collision.

"Hell of a party," Erin said, managing a watery smile and sidestepping the bewildered teen.

The kitchen was slightly less crowded than the living room and Erin saw Forster at once. The jock was talking urgently to a scrawny, greasy-haired guy who was sporting a terrible attempt at a mustache and goatee. Forster was pointing toward the door. Both he and the other kid looked Erin's way and made eye contact with her.

"That's her!" Forster yelped. He shoved the other kid, whom Erin assumed to be Xander Yates, to one side and ran the other way. The kitchen had a back door, which was open, and a thin glass-paned outer door, which wasn't. Forster hit the glass full tilt. The glass was tempered, so it resisted the impact, but the hinges and woodwork were less sturdy. The whole door tore loose. Forster tumbled out of sight down the back steps with a cry that cut off with the sound of breaking glass as the door hit the concrete and shattered.

The other guy, seeing Erin coming toward him and blocking his escape route, scrambled up on the kitchen counter. He fumbled with the latch on the window over the sink, got it open, and was actually halfway out the window by the time she laid hold of his ankle. She yanked him back into the room. The kid clutched at the windowsill. Erin tugged harder with her left hand. With her right, she pressed the X-26 against the boy's calf and let him have about a second's worth of portable lightning.

The kid screamed and let go of the sill. Erin hauled him down to the floor, leaving him face down on the linoleum. She planted a knee in the small of his back and leaned down to talk into his ear.

"Xander Yates?" she said.

"I didn't do it!" the kid protested.

"I'm going to check your pockets," Erin said. "Any needles or sharp objects?"

He didn't answer. She patted him down quickly and efficiently, finding a baggie of pills and a roll of cash. She pulled the pills out and dangled them in front of his nose.

"What are these?" she asked rhetorically. "Allergy medication? Jelly beans?"

Yates kept quiet, which was probably smart. Erin sighed and adjusted her knee on his back. She had to arrest him, or there was no way to link him to Millhouse. And he definitely deserved to be arrested. But this was going to ruin not only his night and hers, but Lieutenant Webb's and Campus Security Chief Oglesby's, too.

Erin took out her phone and called Dispatch. "This is Detective O'Reilly, shield four-six-four-oh," she said. "I need a Patrol unit to the Sigma Nu house at Columbia. Got one in custody, possibly another nearby. You'd better send a bus, too." Over the sounds of the party that filtered in from the living room, she could hear Forster moaning. Tempered glass was designed to shatter into small pebbles instead of big, jagged shards, so he was probably pretty much okay, but they'd need to get him checked out. Erin had caused enough trouble already, without indirectly killing a would-be date-rapist.

Something wet and sticky trickled into her eyes. She put up a hand and realized her forehead was bleeding. What a perfect end to a perfect night.

Chapter 13

Erin hauled Xander Yates into the interrogation room, tossed him unceremoniously into the chair, and slammed the door. He was still wearing the handcuffs she'd borrowed from one of the Patrol uniforms who'd arrived as backup. She'd gotten away from Columbia as fast as she could, leaving a trail of flashing lights, cops, and chattering students in her wake.

She hadn't bothered to change her clothes, or even bandage the cut on her face. The drying blood and smeared makeup gave her a savage appearance. Yates shrank away from her. He was a small guy and his fear made him seem smaller.

"Okay, Xander," she snarled. "Start talking."

"About what?" he stammered. "Those pills aren't anything. They're just, like, allergy medication."

"We're going to test them, you know," she said. "If you're carrying it around, Rohypnol will get you charged with criminal possession. But with your pal Royal in custody, you're looking at criminal sale of a controlled substance. Because I'm guessing that girl he dosed up earlier this evening is coasting on pills you provided. And that makes you an accessory to attempted rape, too."

"Hey, whatever he did with that shit is on him, not on me. It's not my fault." Yates adopted an air of wounded innocence that was about as convincing as if he'd been a fox in a henhouse, bloody feathers all over his mouth.

"You came to college to get an education, right?" Erin said. "Tonight's lesson is about consequences. There's only one way for you to get out of this without going to prison for a really long time, and that's to tell me what I need to know. You ready to play ball?"

"What do you want?" he asked, and Erin knew she had him.

"Christopher Millhouse," she said. "Creepy Chris. You know him? Dark hair, skinny, pale, kind of smug?"

"Yeah, I know him," Yates said.

"Did you sell to him recently?"

"Hey, I don't sell to anybody!"

"Knock it off!" Erin shouted, banging her hand on the table for emphasis. Yates jumped and shrank back again. "Don't give me that crap! We both know exactly what you've been doing, and I don't have time for your bullshit. Give me what you've got, or you're going straight to Riker's Island, right into GenPop, and you can feed the other inmates your excuses. Chris Millhouse; yes or no?"

"I might've given him a couple pills," Yates said. "Maybe."

"When might this have happened?" she demanded.

"At a party. Like, a week ago."

"What'd he want them for?"

"Like I said, that's on him," Yates said. "I don't ask."

"How did he know to come to you? Dealers don't deal to just anybody. Somebody vouched for him."

"He said he was a friend of Royal's," Yates said sulkily. "He said he was pledging Sigma and they had a thing he needed the pills for."

Erin's stomach twisted. She wanted to grab a handful of Yates's greasy hair and bang his face into the tabletop until she knocked some decency into him. "How many pills?" she asked.

"Like, two."

That was what Erin needed. She had a dealer who'd provided drugs to Millhouse. That, combined with Forster's statement, gave evidence of premeditation. It was circumstantial, still not enough for an indictment, but it was progress.

"Okay," she said. "Stand up."

"I gave you what you wanted!" he whined. "You're not throwing me in with the gang members and stuff, are you?"

"You're going into Holding," Erin said grimly. "What happens to you after that is up to the DA."

*   *   *

Now that it was too late to stop, now that she had arrest reports to write and DD-5s to file, the nervous energy that had kept Erin awake had drained away. She dragged herself upstairs to Major Crimes, using the railing to help her up each step in her damn high heels. She had blisters on her feet and her ankles hurt.

The main office was deserted. She felt a momentary gratitude that she wouldn't have to deal with Webb until morning. She'd called him, but her call had gone to voicemail and she'd left the most innocuous message she'd thought she could get away with while still being truthful. Maybe he was still sleeping the sleep of the blissfully ignorant.

Erin was so tired and preoccupied, she didn't notice the light shining under the door of Captain Holliday's office. She slumped in front of her computer and started mechanically going through the motions of the necessary paperwork for the night's adventures. She didn't hear the door open behind her, didn't register anything out of the ordinary until the Captain cleared his throat less than two feet from her.

Every nerve in her body came instantly awake. She leaped out of her chair and spun around, hand reflexively going to her belt. She recognized Holliday at the same moment she remembered she wasn't wearing her Glock. There stood the Captain, fully dressed, necktie neatly knotted, mustache sleek and well-groomed, as if it was the middle of the workday rather than the heart of the dog watch.

"Detective," Holliday said quietly.

"Sir," she said, standing at attention. Now she was fully conscious of her disheveled state. She wished fervently she had two more inches of skirt and five minutes' cleanup in the restroom.

"I'd like a word with you, if you're not too busy."

"Of course, sir."

"In my office."

With a sinking heart, she said, "Yes, sir," and followed him like a naughty schoolgirl who'd been sent to the principal.

Holliday's office shone with a warm, golden light. The Captain's desk was made of lovely red-brown wood, accented with little brass knickknacks. Except for his computer, it felt like a slice of another century. The room had a pleasant, inviting aspect normally absent from police stations. But Erin felt no warmth. Holliday didn't often show temper, but she could feel something cold and icy radiating from him now.

He walked around his desk and sat in his well-worn leather swivel chair. Two more chairs were in front of the desk, but he didn't offer her a seat and she didn't take one. She stood at attention, staring straight ahead, bracing herself for what was coming.

"You've been a detective over a year now," Holliday said, still speaking quietly, politely.

It wasn't a question, so Erin didn't answer.

"And you've worn a shield, what, twelve years?" he continued.

"Yes, sir," she said.

"You're familiar with the Patrol Guide and the rules and regulations of the Department?"

"Yes, sir."

"And you understand that Columbia University's campus police have primary jurisdiction over their student body and campus?"

"Yes, sir." She tried not to sigh as she said it.

Holliday clasped his hands on his desk. "Are you aware that Chief Oglesby is demanding your resignation?"

Erin's heart skipped. She involuntarily broke her stolid stare and looked right into Holliday's eyes. "No!" she exclaimed. "He can't—"

"Nobody can force you to resign, Detective," Holliday said. "But he is within his rights to make the request of the PC. And I understand he has done so, through proper, official channels."

"On what charge, sir?" Erin had recovered some of her composure, but her pulse was hammering. She hoped she wouldn't lose her temper, or burst into angry tears, or say anything stupid.

"He claims you assaulted two students and arrested them without probable cause, deploying your Taser unnecessarily and damaging campus property in the process."

Erin bit her lip and waited. She wanted to speak in her own defense, but Holliday was a fair man. She'd get her say. Better not to interrupt him.

Holliday's mustache twitched as he worked his jaw. "You're a good officer, O'Reilly," he said. "And an excellent detective. So

I'm sure you have your reasons. For your sake, and the Department's, I hope they're good enough. Go on, tell me what happened and why."

"You know about Christopher Millhouse?" she said.

He nodded. "Yes. I also know his father is CEO of Wildfyre, Inc., and is one of the ten wealthiest men in New York."

Erin hadn't known that. "Does that make a difference, sir?" she asked warily.

"Not in my precinct," Holliday said. "But the DA may feel differently. He has to consider politics. So do I, though not to the same degree."

"Millhouse bought drugs from Xander Yates," she said. "Yates just admitted as much to me downstairs. Millhouse pumped Royal Forster for information about the upcoming blackout, and drugged him so he wouldn't remember it."

"So you're building your case against Millhouse," Holliday said. "And the Taser?"

"Forster had a girl with him. He'd drugged her and was in the process of assaulting her. I intervened to protect an innocent and prevent a major felony."

"Columbia is one of the safest campuses in the country," Holliday said. "Chief Oglesby reminded the PC of that, who in turn passed that nugget of knowledge on to me when he called me a short while ago."

"I don't know stats, sir," Erin said stiffly. "But I know what happened tonight. I caught Forster in the act of raping that girl."

"And you have the girl in question and her statement to that effect?"

"No, sir."

"Why not?"

"She was drugged, incoherent, and unable to give a statement. I had two suspects to collar, so I left her in the care of some of her friends." Erin paused. "I don't think she'll be able to give testimony. She was pretty out of it."

"Other witnesses?"

"Nobody who saw it happening. Angie Ordway is the friend who took charge of the victim. She can testify to the girl's condition."

"I will so inform campus police," Holliday said dryly. "And they will follow up on it. You understand, we're not going to be prosecuting Mr. Yates or Mr. Forster."

Erin bristled, but she understood the politics of the situation. "We're letting a rapist walk because of a jurisdiction dispute," she said bitterly.

"A rapist is walking because of decisions made by the officer on scene," Holliday said, a flash of anger finally cutting through his polite façade.

"If I hadn't been there, he would've succeeded in raping her," Erin retorted. "Sir."

"And if you'd liaised properly with campus police in advance, you would have had backup already on scene and we wouldn't be having this conversation," Holliday said sharply. "I'm not here to absolve you of your sins, Detective, or to listen to excuses."

Erin realized she was walking right on the line. "Yes, sir," she said more softly.

"Did you deploy your Taser on Mr. Yates?" Holliday asked.

"Yes, sir. He was trying to escape out the window. I gave him a little jolt, just a second or so. On the leg."

"And Mr. Forster?"

"Him, too."

"Why?"

Erin considered lying, or stretching the truth, but she decided the hell with it. "He'd just dropped his pants and was about to get on top of the victim. So I gave him a contact shock to the groin."

"And that didn't strike you as excessive force?"

"Not in the moment, sir."

"What about now, with the benefit of hindsight?"

"I'd do exactly the same thing again, sir." She thought about it for a moment and added, "Maybe two or three seconds instead of one."

Holliday didn't quite crack a smile, but his mustache quivered. "I see," he said. "This leaves us with something of an awkward situation."

"Yes, sir."

"Take a breath, O'Reilly. I'm not going to ask for your shield. Not even a suspension. At least, not tonight."

Erin's heart leaped. She swallowed the thanks that tried to gush out of her mouth and maintained her professional decorum.

"The incident will, of course, be referred to IAB," Holliday went on. "And there may be consequences. It will definitely go on your record. But there will be no rush to summary judgment. For now, you will continue with your normal duties. As long as those duties keep you clear of Columbia campus. That area is off-limits to you until further notice. Are we clear?"

"Crystal, sir."

"I'll speak to your squad commander," he said. "That will be all, Detective. Please close the door when you go."

"Thank you, sir." Erin saluted. Then she left his office and shut the door. She felt shaky. She hadn't realized just how close a shave she'd had. She'd risked everything with hardly a second thought: the undercover operation against the O'Malleys, her relationship with Carlyle, her career, even Rolf. And it was still hanging over her, like an executioner's axe. Holliday hadn't said it, but there'd been an implied threat. If she didn't nail

Millhouse, if she didn't prove this was worth it, the consequences might be more personal than letting a killer go free. If this case fell apart, it might drag her down with it.

* * *

A couple of hours and many pages of paperwork later, utterly drained, Erin shuffled into the Barley Corner by way of the back door. The pub had closed at two and the front door was locked. The main room was dark, lit only by the streetlights through the blinds. In the dim, slanting light, the upside-down chairs on top of the tables looked like the broken pillars of some ancient ruin.

Erin was already reaching for the keypad to open the apartment door when she paused. She hadn't seen any movement, but her gut told her she wasn't alone. She forced herself to focus and scanned the room slowly, sliding a hand into her purse and feeling for her .38.

He was sitting at the bar, half-hidden by the shadow of a window-frame, sitting very still. Erin's adrenal system dumped its last dregs into her bloodstream. She yanked out the pistol and took aim.

"NYPD," she said to the dark shape. "You're trespassing. I'm tired, I'm pissed, I'm armed, and I've had a lousy night, so whatever you're thinking of trying, don't."

The shadowy man cocked his head in an oddly familiar way. He slowly opened his hands, showing empty palms.

"Don't you get tired of pointing weapons at me, Erin?" Corky Corcoran asked softly. "That's twice in the past twenty-four hours. Do it again and I'll start thinking you don't like me. Now, if you'd not mind turning on one of those wee lights beside you? Just one, mind. No sense advertising our presence to the whole neighborhood."

"Corky," Erin sighed. She lowered the pistol and reached for the light switches, flicking on the one that lit the bar. A little island of light flickered and formed around Corky. He was sitting halfway down the bar, two shot glasses and a half-empty bottle of Glen D whiskey in front of him. He looked tired, but calm.

Erin crossed the room and stood next to his stool, tucking the .38 back into her handbag. "All right," she said. "What're you doing here?"

"Your lad doesn't mind if I stay after closing," Corky said. "No need to bother about me. I'll let myself out."

"I can't believe Carlyle leaves you unsupervised in a room full of his liquor," Erin said.

"There's only so much a lad can drink at one go," he replied. "Sit down, join me for a glass. Your lover's footing the bill."

"Corky, I was telling the truth. I've had a shitty night."

"So I can tell," he said, letting his eyes rove over her face. "I'd hate to see the other lad. All the more reason to take a glass before bed. Keeps the bad dreams off."

"I'm really not in the mood for more bullshit tonight," she said. "Whatever this is—"

"Sit down," he said. "Please. I've been waiting for you half the bloody night."

That caught her attention; not so much what he said at the end, but the magic word. She couldn't ever recall hearing Corky use the word "please."

Erin nodded and slid onto the stool. "Okay. Pour me one."

Corky filled both glasses with a generous splash of fine whiskey. In the light over the bar it shone like liquid gold. He hoisted his glass.

"*Slainte*," he said.

Erin let him clink his glass against hers. She took a sip, enjoying the familiar burn in her throat. "You were waiting for me," she said. "Here I am. What's so important?"

"It's not important to me," he said. "But it seems to matter the devil of a lot to you. I've been thinking on what you asked of me."

Erin held up a hand. "Look, Corky, I'm sorry. I didn't mean it that way."

He nodded. "Aye, love. I know. And I'm sorry for taking offense. You'll recall I'd just been in Vicky's company."

"Yeah. She was all over you."

"That she was, and I'm thinking we both know why." He gulped down the rest of his drink and immediately poured another. "Vicky's scared. She'd tied herself to Mickey Connor, thinking he was the coming man. When he went down, she was cast loose to fend for herself. She's attracted to strength. Perhaps I should be flattered, since she so clearly thinks my star's on the rise, but in truth, she made me feel cheap. Used. I didn't much care for it."

"You knew she was using you," Erin said, nodding.

"I'm no eejit," Corky said. "She's a cute hoor, no doubt about it."

"She's some kind of whore," Erin said.

"Nay, that's not what I meant," he said, waving a hand vaguely in front of his face. "Sometimes when I get fluthered, I fall back on the slang I knew when I was a wee lad. A cute hoor is someone who works on others to get what they want. A manipulator, you ken?"

"Okay," Erin said. "I get it. But what does 'fluthered' mean?"
"Drunk."

"I've seen you drink. Not sure I've ever seen you drunk."

"You're seeing it now," he said. "But as I was saying, when you came to me with your hand out, I took it the worst way I could. Here's the long and short of it, Erin. I did your kin a bad turn a ways back and I'm sorry for it. I'm doing what I can to make amends. You want to know what Maggie Callahan knows? All right, I'll find out for you. Word of honor. But I'll do it my own way, in my own time. And I'll do nothing to harm her. She's living with wolves, aye, but she's naught but a wee lamb herself."

Corky laughed softly and took another drink. "This stuff's making me sentimental. You'll forgive me for that, aye?"

"Aye," Erin said. Then she blinked. "I mean, yeah. Of course. Your accent's contagious, did you know that?"

"Sexiest in the world," he said solemnly. "Oh, some will tell you the English have it better, but which do you prefer?"

"I'm biased," she said. "But Irish, of course."

"It's a fool's errand anyway, trying to seduce Maggie," he said. "She's no interest at all in that sort of thing."

"You think she's gay?" Erin asked. It wouldn't surprise her.

"Nor that neither," he said. "Nay, she's simply not interested. Some folk are wired that way. Never understood it myself, but that's the world for you."

"So how do you plan on getting to her?"

"I plan on being her friend," Corky said.

"That's all, huh? You think it'll be that easy?"

"I think it'll be bloody hard," he retorted. "If it were easy, you'd have already done it yourself."

"Good point. But we don't have endless amounts of time."

"That's been true from the moment we were born," he said. "And we've less time every second. Nothing's changed. Friendship might be easier than seduction, in some ways, but I'll have to move carefully. I can't let Evan catch wind of what I'm on about, or you'll be needing to find a new drinking companion."

"It's not enough to know she's Evan's accountant," Erin reminded him. "We need the numbers. All of them. What makes you think she'll just tell you?"

He smiled and his green eyes took on some of their accustomed sparkle. "You're doubting me, love?"

"No," she sighed. "I'm just worried. I had a close call tonight. Everything's so damn fragile. This could all come crashing down any moment. It could happen tomorrow, for all I know."

"What happened?" he asked, laying a hand on hers. To her surprise, Erin felt no sense from his touch that he was looking for physical intimacy. He was just acting the part of a concerned friend. Maybe he could handle Maggie after all.

"Oh, the usual," she said. "I beat up some perps and the Captain threatened to throw me off the Force."

"You can't follow all the rules all the time," he said.

"And you can't follow any of them anytime," she shot back. "But thanks for doing this, Corky. It means a lot."

"Well, since it means so very much to you, I'll take the rest of the bottle with me," he said, plucking it from the bar and slipping off his stool. "And with that, I'll bid you goodnight, love."

"Goodnight, Corky."

He puckered his lips and blew her an airy kiss. Then he winked and turned for the door.

Chapter 14

About two seconds after Erin's head hit the pillow, her alarm was going off in her ear and it was time to dig in again. At least, that was what it felt like. She'd actually managed to grab about three hours of sleep. She'd had to shower before bed, and as a result, she woke up clean, but her hair was a tangled mess.

Carlyle, beside her, made a muffled sound and rolled over. He'd lived by night for so many years, he'd learned to tune out lights and sounds in the morning. She gave him an envious look. Then Rolf was standing at the bedside, tail swishing, ears fully perked, ready for their morning run.

She didn't want to go. Her muscles felt like she'd been beaten with two-by-fours and her head was pounding much worse than the shot of whiskey really warranted. But Sean O'Reilly's daughter hadn't been raised to do the easy thing. Besides, she owed Rolf for abandoning him the previous night. So she got up and put on her running clothes.

The run cleared her head a little. Coming back sweaty, she hopped in the shower again. This time, she was awake enough to take a moment to examine her shoulder in the bathroom mirror. The tattoo wasn't as bad as she'd feared. It was actually kind of attractive; an intricate Celtic knot, about two inches across.

"Could be worse," she muttered. Still tired, she got dressed and went across the street to the parking garage, had her K-9 do a quick check of her car just in case somebody had planted a bomb on the undercarriage, loaded Rolf into the back, and drove to work.

She found Webb and Vic in Major Crimes. One glance at Webb's face told Erin that he'd had a conversation with Holliday. He looked older and sourer than usual.

"Heard you had some fun last night," Vic said.

"Those two guys you brought in have been released," Webb said. "No charges."

Erin nodded. It was what she'd expected and there was no point complaining. "What about Millhouse?" she asked.

"He's still here," Webb said. "When I went down to Holding, he pointed at the clock over the door and smiled. Tell me you've got something to wipe that smile off his face. He's starting to get on my nerves."

"Hold on a sec," Vic said. "I heard it from the guy who had the front desk last night that Erin came in dressed like a hooker and looking like she'd been in a bitch-fight. She was dragging a pair of jocks, one in each hand. I want details."

"That situation's been resolved," Webb said.

"Where were you?" Vic pressed, refusing to be deflected.

"At a frat party," she said. "Chasing leads and getting in fights with idiots."

"And you didn't think to bring me?" Vic asked. He looked hurt.

"It was a spur-of-the-moment thing," Erin said.

"And without the knowledge or permission of campus security," Webb added.

"You definitely should've brought me, in that case," Vic said. "What'd the two mopes do?"

"Attempted rape and drug dealing," Erin said.

"What'd you do to the rapist?"

"Tased him in the nuts."

Vic grinned. "Outstanding."

Webb scowled. "Not helping, Neshenko. Just because O'Reilly hasn't been suspended yet doesn't mean she won't be."

"I used to get detention all the time in grade school," Vic said.

"Your previous CO's reasons for approving your transfer out of his squad become clearer with every passing day," Webb said. "Now, if you'd care to do some police work, we've got a self-described murderer downstairs who's going to be back on the street in a little over twenty-four hours unless one of you can come up with a reason to hold him that'll satisfy a judge. Suggestions?"

"I want to go back to the construction site," Erin said.

"It's been contaminated," Webb said. "We didn't have it cordoned off. And you already checked it."

"I want to check it again," she said. "We missed something. I think the body's still there."

"And you know this because...?" Webb prompted.

"Intuition," she said.

"Women's intuition?" Vic asked with a sardonic smile.

"No," she said. "Detective's intuition. Another type you apparently know nothing about. Also, I think Rolf smelled it, but Millhouse must've spilled bleach on site. I missed it with all the other chemical smells at the scene, but it would've prevented Rolf from sniffing the body. I think she's buried under the site."

"I want to brace Millhouse again," Vic said. "See if we can shake him."

"And I think we should look deeper into the alleged victim," Webb said. "Let's keep trying to contact her, just in case she's still alive. But first, I want you two talking to our resident nut case. Once you're done with him, then you can go kick dirt around."

*　　*　　*

"I hate him," Vic said as they went down the stairs.

"He's got a lot to put up with," Erin said. "And we aren't making it easy on him."

"I don't want to make it easy on him! Why the hell would I want to do that? He deserves every bit of shit we can throw at him!"

She paused on the landing. "That's a little harsh, don't you think, Vic?"

"You're *defending* this asshole?" he exclaimed, drawing startled looks from a pair of uniforms on the ground floor.

"He's just doing his job," Erin said. "And he's not out to get us, even if it feels that way sometimes."

"Wait a second," he said. "I was talking about Millhouse. You thought I meant..."

"The Lieutenant."

"Oh. Yeah, I kinda hate him too. But that's in my professional capacity. I hate this kid on a personal level. He gives me the creeps."

"So you're saying you want to play bad cop when we talk to him?"

"Yeah. You got a problem with that?"

She shook her head. "It's what you were born to do, Vic."

Chris Millhouse was standing perfectly still in the middle of his cell, hands at his sides, back straight. It would've been creepy if Erin hadn't recognized the pose. He was doing an

Anthony Hopkins impression from *Silence of the Lambs*, and Hopkins had done it better. Knowing that just made the whole thing seem phony and a little pathetic. But the smile he gave them when they approached almost made up for it.

"Good morning, Detectives," he said. "How may I help you?"

"Turn around, hands through the slot," Vic said, taking out his cuffs.

"You're not scared of me, are you?" Millhouse asked. "You must weigh twice as much as I do. Besides, you have her to back you up."

"You kidding?" Vic shot back. "This is for your protection, not mine. If I don't follow procedure, you might try to make a run for it or start a fight, and then I'd have to break your leg, or dislocate both your shoulders, or put you in an illegal chokehold. I don't need the extra paperwork, and you're not worth it. Hands. Now."

"He's very rude," Millhouse said to Erin. "Is he like that in the bedroom, too?"

Erin didn't even bother to answer. The suggestion that a female cop must be sleeping with her male colleagues was about as tired a cliché as there was. Back in her Patrol days, she'd heard that and worse from drunks at least once a shift.

Millhouse offered no physical resistance as they cuffed him and steered him to the interrogation room. He still seemed amused by everything. He sat in the steel chair, hands shackled behind him, and just kept smiling.

"You think this is funny?" Vic challenged, leaning over the table. "We'll see if you're still smiling in maximum security, when three hundred pounds of tattooed convict rolls out the welcome wagon for the fresh meat that's sharing his cell."

"Take it easy, Vic," Erin said, laying a hand on his arm. "Remember, Chris came here voluntarily. He wants to help us."

"Take it easy," Millhouse repeated. "You don't want to put any undue strain on yourself. Did you know that police officers are at the highest risk of suicide of any occupation in America? Studies suggest it's due to the high stress of your job, the high instances of post-traumatic stress, and easy access to loaded firearms."

"I wouldn't give a little punk like you the satisfaction," Vic said. "I plan on enjoying my retirement, thinking about all the shitbirds I put behind bars."

"Thank you for telling us where you killed Annmarie," Erin said, using the name deliberately, hoping for a reaction. "It was a big help to our investigation."

Millhouse glanced at her. "Oh, was that her name?" he asked. "That's funny. I have a professor with the same first name."

"That's because they're the same person, jerkoff!" Vic growled. "And you planned the whole thing from the start. You're not fooling anybody."

"It sounds like you have everything you need, then," Millhouse said. "If you've identified the victim, I don't think I can be of any further assistance."

"It was a smart move using bleach," Erin said. "You must've thought this through pretty carefully."

"I've thought of everything," Millhouse said. "So my question for you is, how far over the line have you already gone, and how far are you going to go?"

"What do you mean?" Erin asked, more sharply than she meant to.

"You can't prove anything by following your rulebook," he said. "So either you're going to give up or you're going to break the rules. It doesn't matter which. You won't get me either way. But I look forward to seeing which way you go. I'd guess your big friend would like to beat something out of me, but there's two problems with that. It'd be illegal, which would mean I'd be let go immediately, with a damage settlement against the NYPD, and since I've already confessed, I don't even know what he'd be trying to get me to say."

Erin stared at him, fighting down the urge to punch him herself. His smug self-assurance was maddening. "Looks like you've got us dead to rights," she said, keeping her tone light and conversational. "What gave you the idea of hiding the body under the concrete?"

"I think I've said everything I want to say," Millhouse said. "I'll give you three choices, Detectives. You can let me walk out the front door right now, you can take me back to my room for another... let's say, twenty-three hours and change, or you can give me the benefit of the highly-paid legal counsel my father will be delighted to provide."

"Chris, if you don't help me, I can't help you," Erin said, but she'd lost this round and they both knew it. He'd called her bluff and her cards just weren't quite strong enough.

"He wants to go back in his cell, I say we put him back in his cell," Vic said. "Preferably head-first."

Erin nodded. "If that's what he wants, it's what he'll get."

*   *   *

"Waste of time," Vic said sourly. "God! How could you keep talking to that creep?"

They were back in Major Crimes, with Millhouse safe in his holding cell. Webb was at his computer, ignoring them.

"I seduced a serial killer in our interrogation room once," Erin reminded him. "It's all part of the game. This guy's guilty, Vic."

"Yeah, so he's been telling us. For all the good it's done. He thinks he's gonna walk."

"And he's right," she said. "Damn him. I'm getting desperate and it's making me sloppy. I'm breaking rules."

Vic snapped his fingers. "Just like he said. Maybe that's the whole point! Like the guy in *Seven*, trying to make a cop into a killer."

"This isn't a movie, Vic." She paused. "Wait a second, maybe it is. You saw him doing his Hopkins impression, didn't you?"

"You think we're in a movie?" Vic raised an eyebrow.

"No. But Millhouse is playing a role and he's going off what he knows. He sees these super-smart serial killers playing games with the cops, so that's what he decides to do. You want to know what this guy's motivation is? I think he's just bored."

"He's not as smart as he thinks he is," Vic said. "They never are. I've never met a perfect criminal."

"Of course not," she said. "If they were perfect, you'd never know about them. They'd never get caught."

He scowled. "Okay, Little Miss Smartass, let me tell you something—"

The buzz of Erin's phone interrupted him. She gave him an artificial smile and held up a finger while she took out the phone. The screen showed an out-of-state area code.

"O'Reilly," she said.

"Ma'am?" The voice was polite but worried. "This is Damien... Damien Hilton. You gave me this number and told me to call you if I heard anything."

"Yes," she said, gripping the phone more tightly. "Thanks for getting back to me, Mr. Hilton. What did you hear?"

"I got an e-mail from Annmarie," he said.

"When was it sent?" Erin asked. Her head was spinning. She brought up the recording app on her phone and set it in motion, taping the conversation.

"Two nights ago. I found it in my inbox this morning, just a few minutes ago. I'm sorry I didn't check it sooner. But it was my work e-mail and I've been home. I've just been so busy. We have a new baby, you see, and..."

"What did it say?" she interrupted.

"It... it looked like... like a suicide note."

"Can you forward that e-mail to me? Immediately?" Erin lunged for her desk.

"Of course," Damien said. "Just give me your address."

Erin rattled it off. While Damien sent the e-mail, Erin snapped her fingers at Vic.

"What?" he said.

She muted her phone. "Ping Annmarie Hilton's cell," she said. "Right now."

The e-mail showed up on her screen. It was short and to the point.

I've done something terrible and I can't live with myself any longer. Goodbye. Annmarie.

"Did you get it?" Damien asked anxiously.

Erin unmuted the phone. "Yes, thank you," she said.

"Does... does this have anything to do with your call?" he asked. "Did you find, you know, a body?"

Not yet, and that's the problem, Erin thought. She said, "No. But we're trying our best to locate your sister. Are you sure that e-mail came from her?"

"Of course it did," Damien said. "It's from her e-mail."

"But might someone else have been using that e-mail account?" Erin asked.

"I can't think who," he said. "But it's a little strange. It's probably nothing, but..."

"Tell me, please." Detectives loved details that didn't fit. Those were the ones that broke cases.

"Ever since she moved to New York, she'd been signing her e-mails 'NY Hilton.' It was a joke. You know, like Paris Hilton, only a different city."

"But this one is signed 'Annmarie,'" Erin said.

"That's right," Damien said. "But... if she didn't send it, who did?"

"That's what we're trying to determine. Is this all you received?"

"Yes. Ma'am, please... tell me the truth. Is my sister dead?"

"I can't answer that at this time," Erin said, hating the words as they left her mouth. "But I promise to call you as soon as we know. Thank you, Mr. Hilton."

Erin looked up as she ended the call. Vic was on his feet, excited. Rolf was up too, wagging and eager.

"Got a hit on the cell," Vic announced.

"Where?" Erin asked.

"GPS puts it on the East River Promenade, right by the Williamsburg Bridge."

Webb hurried over to join them. "Let's go," he said. "Have Dispatch send a couple units to canvass the area, in case the body's there."

"It isn't," Erin said.

"You sure of that?" Vic asked.

She shook her head helplessly. She wasn't sure of anything at the moment.

* * *

The Williamsburg Bridge towered over the East River Park, an overarching thicket of crisscrossing gray steel girders. Four uniformed officers were standing around, poking through shrubs and peering into trash cans. A few curious New Yorkers watched them without much interest.

"Where's the signal?" Webb asked.

"Somewhere around the base of that support column," Vic said, pointing to a cluster of brush. "Got it within ten meters or so."

"Rolf, *such*," Erin said, aiming the K-9 at the indicated patch of ground.

Rolf sniffed his way over, nostrils flaring. He was trained to detect explosives, people, and cadavers. If Annmarie Hilton was lying there, he'd find her. The Shepherd raised his head, gave a few experimental snuffles, and continued his search, but Erin knew her partner's body language and could sense his uncertainty.

"No corpse," she said after a few moments.

"Especially if she took a header off the bridge," Vic said. "I don't care how soft this ground is, she'd have made a mess coming down. Like a watermelon hitting pavement."

"Yuck," Erin said.

"Hey, you wanted to investigate homicides," he said. "It's gross when people die."

Rolf paused and poked his snout into an ornamental bush. Erin glanced at it and saw a glimmer of light reflecting off a polished surface.

"Over here!" she said. "Looks like a phone."

Webb pulled on a pair of gloves and carefully reached into the bush, drawing out a phone. "I think I see bloodstains on this," he said, turning it over. "Not very pronounced. Looks like it's been wiped down. But I can see it in the cracks around the protective case. That doesn't make sense if she tossed it away and then jumped."

"Annmarie didn't commit suicide," Erin said. "She didn't send that e-mail and she didn't put that phone there."

"I understand what you're saying," Webb said. "But we have to check."

"I guess the Harbor Patrol's going to drag the river," Vic said.

"We don't have time for that!" Erin protested. "It'll take hours, and they won't find anything anyway!"

"It's the East River," Vic said. "There's bodies all over the place down there. The Mob dump dead guys here all the time. They might find *somebody*."

"Don't you see what he's doing, sir?" Erin asked Webb. "He's creating doubt, making us chase our tails and waste time, making us look stupid."

"If that's his plan, he's succeeding," Webb said. "You had Ms. Hilton declared missing. Now we have to follow up on our best lead as to her whereabouts, which is this phone and its message."

"Its phony message," she insisted.

"If she was murdered and the message was forged, then her killer was here," he said. "And there may be other clues."

"The phone isn't damaged," Vic said. "Lucky, falling all that way. But how did our boy get all the way here from the murder site during the power outage?"

"The *presumed* murder site," Webb corrected.

"He probably didn't," Erin said. "Nobody was looking for Annmarie at that point. He had all night. He could've just taken her phone with him and come here any time before he walked into the Eightball."

"What about the blood on the phone?" Vic asked.

Erin had been thinking about that. "Let's dust it for prints," she said. "Just on the off-chance. Then I need to check something."

The fingerprint powder, unsurprisingly, turned up no prints on the screen.

"Wiped down, like I said," Webb muttered.

"Okay," Erin said. She peeled off her glove and swiped her fingertip across the screen. The phone lit up. A message requested that she press her finger against the screen to unlock the phone. She did so. The phone remained locked.

"Biometric security," Webb said.

"And that's why the blood," Erin said.

"You mean... Jesus Christ," Vic said. "Pruning shears."

"Or a knife, or whatever," she agreed. "He took one of her fingers."

"That sick son of a bitch," Vic said. "So now we're looking for a finger?"

"Worth a look," Erin said. "Rolf should be able to find it. He can find whole bodies, so pieces shouldn't be too hard."

"We'll want to get this phone back to the lab, in case our techs can pull any data off it," Webb said. "I agree, this doesn't look like a suicide."

But in spite of that, Erin thought grimly, they were still looking in the wrong place. And the clock was still ticking.

Chapter 15

The idea of finding a single finger in a New York park was absurd on the face of it, a real needle-in-a-haystack situation. How to find the proverbial needle was one of the classic questions. Erin knew the clever answers; use a magnet or set fire to the hay. But she figured the best way was to get a K-9 who knew what the needle smelled like.

They didn't have Annmarie Hilton's body or clothing to work with, but they did have her phone, and on the phone was her blood. Only small traces, true, but that was more than Rolf needed. One sniff at the phone and the Shepherd was off. They started where the phone had landed and worked outward, quartering the ground. Webb, Vic, and the Patrol officers did what they could to help, but Erin trusted Rolf's nose more than all their eyes.

The K-9 alerted a few feet from the riverbank, scratching the grass and whining. Erin knelt down beside him and saw a small, pale thing lying on the ground. Careful not to disturb it, she bent closer and examined it. It was, as she'd expected, a human finger, probably the index finger. The nail was carefully manicured and painted with pale pink nail polish.

Erin had seen dozens of dead bodies, people who had died in all sorts of horrible ways. It was one of the things you got used to on the Job. But that one finger affected her. She felt a surge of mingled pity and nausea. That this one part of Annmarie was all they could find seemed like some sort of obscenity, almost as if her killer was flipping them off.

"Good work, O'Reilly," Webb said quietly. He and Vic had come up behind her and were looking over her shoulder.

"He tossed it toward the river," she said in a dull monotone. "But it fell a little short. Otherwise we wouldn't have found it."

"Probably," Webb agreed. "Now we just need to verify that it's hers."

"Because there's so many severed fingers lying around New York?" Vic asked. "Is this some sort of new crime epidemic I haven't heard about? Who else could it be?"

Rolf cocked his head at Erin and wagged his tail uncertainly. He thought he'd been a good boy, but wasn't completely sure. This wasn't a whole person. Maybe he ought to keep looking.

"*Sei brav,*" Erin told Rolf, handing him his chew-toy.

Rolf joyfully grabbed it from her, plopped down on the grass, and rolled over on his back, kicking his paws in the air and wriggling as he chewed, his tail sweeping the grass.

"*Now* can we call Annmarie Hilton a murder victim?" Erin asked.

"You can live without a finger," Webb said. "But I agree, it's not looking good."

"Yeah," Vic said. "Too bad he didn't cut her head off and leave it lying around. Kidding!" he hastily added as Erin shot him a dirty look.

"The ground's pretty soft here," Erin said. "I'd expect footprints if he'd come close."

Webb looked up at the bridge. "Right," he said. "It was almost certainly dropped or thrown down, along with the phone. The phone was heavier, so it fell pretty much straight down. The finger carried a little further. No point having CSU all over the park. And I agree, there's no point dragging the river now."

Erin put her gloves back on and carefully picked up the finger. Vic held out an evidence bag.

"Just a second," she said. "Can I see the phone, sir?"

Webb handed it over. Fighting back the sick feeling deep in her gut, Erin turned the finger over and held its tip to the screen of Annmarie's phone. The phone unlocked immediately.

"That's her all right," Vic said.

Erin slipped the severed digit into the evidence bag, which Vic promptly sealed. He held it up and examined it clinically.

"Doc Levine can say for sure," he said. "But I don't think that's a knife cut. Look, the kerf marks are angled on both sides. That's gotta be either some big-ass scissors, or maybe bolt cutters."

"Bolt cutters," Erin repeated. "Vic, remember the construction site? The gate wasn't locked."

"Yeah. So?"

"The foreman said something about it," she said. "It was supposed to be locked."

Vic nodded. "Okay, yeah, I see what you're saying. You think he cut open the gate. Bolt cutters would be just the thing."

"Why would he bother?" Webb asked. "He said he killed Hilton on spur of the moment. Why break into the construction site at all?"

"To get the rebar he used to whack her," Vic suggested.

"That's an improvised weapon," Erin said. "There'd be no point breaking in just to grab a piece of steel. He could've just smacked her with the bolt cutters themselves."

"So what're you getting at?" Vic asked.

"He needed a place to stash the body," she said. "The body is still at the construction site. I'm sure of it."

"Interesting theory," Webb said. "But we can't get a court order to start digging up foundations based on a theory. We need evidence."

"Then let's get back to the site and find some," she said.

*   *   *

Erin and Rolf were in her Charger, Vic and Webb following in Vic's Taurus. Erin pulled up to the construction site, put the car in park, and then just sat there, staring.

The lot swarmed with hard-hatted workers. The earsplitting rattle of machinery filled the air. A cement mixer had backed up to the entrance, its big cylinder rotating, churning the cement.

Behind her, Vic stopped his car and got out. After a few more seconds, Erin and Webb joined him.

"Son of a bitch," Vic said, almost in a whisper. He put his hands on his hips and shook his head. "I guess they found the money to keep building."

Erin recovered a little. She started walking toward the site. Then, after a few steps, she broke into a run. Vic and Webb followed her. Rolf, temporarily forgotten in his compartment, barked a protest. Erin paused just long enough to pop the Charger's quick-release button. The K-9 leaped out and streaked after her, catching up easily and pacing her.

"Whoa, lady," a construction worker said, stepping across Erin's path. "You can't come in here. It's dangerous."

She held up her shield impatiently. "NYPD Major Crimes," she snapped. "Where's Ledbetter?"

"I'll get him," the man said. "You gotta stay right there, got it? You could get hurt."

Ledbetter was a short distance away, watching a forklift move a stack of I-beams. When the other man spoke to him, he turned toward Erin. She saw the recognition in his face. He hurried over.

"What're you doing here, Lady?" he asked. "You didn't find nothing last time."

"What's going on?" she asked, gesturing toward the workers.

"We got the word yesterday," he said. "The project's back on. Got the guys in this morning."

"Why now?"

"Hey, I don't ask no questions as long as my salary gets paid," he said.

"There's a dead body on this site," she said.

"No, there ain't," he said. "You looked, remember? Listen, I can't shut down. We just got going again. I got a job to do here."

Vic and Webb arrived, having been slowed by Webb's poor physique. Vic scowled at the foreman.

"I've got a job to do, too," Erin said. "I can get a court order, if you want to make this official."

It was a bluff. She didn't think they had enough for a court order.

"I guess you better do that," Ledbetter said. "If I gotta explain this to my boss, I better have a piece of paper to cover my ass."

Vic was examining the gate while Erin and Ledbetter were talking. He waved the others over.

"You got a new padlock here," he said.

"Yeah," Ledbetter said. "The old one got busted. I found it yesterday evening."

"Where is it now?" Erin asked.

"Dumpster," Ledbetter said, waving to the big trailer-sized container that stood on one corner of the lot.

"I knew it," Vic growled. "I friggin' knew it. Can't close a case until somebody digs around in the trash."

"At least it won't be as nasty as some trash bins," Erin said. "It'll be mostly construction debris. Dry, solid stuff. Just watch out for sharp pieces of metal."

"What do you need the lock for?" Ledbetter asked, bewildered.

"Would it be all right if my detectives looked through the trash?" Webb asked politely. "They'll stay out of your way."

"There's a liability issue," Ledbetter said. "What if something falls on them, or they get cut?"

"Forget about that," Vic said. "I signed my life away when I joined the NYPD. I get hurt on the Job, I'm not suing anybody. I've signed waivers like you wouldn't believe."

"Okay," Ledbetter said grudgingly. "But everybody wears a hard hat. That's the rules. Even the dog."

"You've got dog-sized hard hats?" Erin asked, surprised.

A few minutes later, with Rolf wearing a human hard hat jury-rigged to his head with duct tape, the detectives moved around the edge of the construction area to the dumpster. The three cops looked at it dubiously.

"Rock-paper-scissors?" Vic offered.

"You two fight it out," Webb said. "RHIP."

"RHIP?" Erin asked.

"Rank Hath Its Privileges," Webb explained. "Which means I don't have to go up to my elbows in other people's trash if I've got subordinates to do it for me."

Erin turned to Vic. "One... two... three," she counted. On "three" she extended one hand, palm held flat. Simultaneously, Vic put out a fist.

"Paper beats rock," she said.

"Damn," Vic said. "Lucky guess."

"Not really," she said. "You're a rock kind of guy. I bet you pick rock the first nine times out of ten, and the other one, you pick scissors. Never paper."

"You know it," he said, grabbing the rim of the bin and pulling himself up and over. It was about six feet tall, so Erin and Webb couldn't see what Vic was doing, but the string of crashes, clanks, and curses told them he was sifting through the debris.

It took almost twenty minutes, but then one of Vic's gloved hands appeared above the rim, triumphantly clutching a padlock with a broken hasp. He climbed out again, filthy but smiling grimly.

"It's been cut," he said, holding it out for their inspection.

"By a bolt cutter," Webb agreed.

"By the same bolt cutter?" Erin wondered aloud.

"I don't know," Vic said. "But I bet Levine could compare them."

He took out the evidence bag from the East River Park and held it up next to the lock. "Angle looks pretty similar," he said.

"Holy shit," Ledbetter said. "Is that a *finger*? You've got a fuckin' finger in your pocket?"

"Or we could just look at the blood on the metal," Erin said, ignoring the foreman. "Look!"

There were little flecks of brown on the bright, fresh metal of the cut. An uninformed observer would have thought they were rust, but the detectives knew better.

Webb produced an evidence bag. "Excellent," he said. Vic dropped the lock into the bag.

The Lieutenant turned to Ledbetter. "Sir," he said. "That lock and that blood, coupled with other evidence we acquired earlier today, constitute probable cause for a murder having been committed on these premises, night before last. I'll get you your court order, but your people may be damaging or destroying evidence this very minute. We need to examine this site again, immediately. Please."

Ledbetter thought it over. "Okay," he said. "I'll call a coffee break. It'll give you fifteen or twenty to take a look around. That's the best I can do."

"Thank you," Webb said.

The foreman blew a whistle and called his men to stop what they were doing. The workers stopped happily enough, filtering away from the work site in search of refreshments. Erin, Vic, Webb, and Rolf, still wearing their hats, started searching.

"Wildfyre," Erin said as Rolf did his sniffing.

"Millhouse's father," Webb said. "He's the CEO. Why didn't you tell me this was a company site?"

"I didn't know it mattered," Erin said. "I didn't know about Millhouse's dad at the time. I didn't even notice the sign."

"You think he knew about this place?" Vic asked.

"I don't see how it could be a coincidence," she said. "He easily could've known the construction had stalled, and he might have also known it would start up again soon."

"That's why he picked this location," Vic said. "Easy body disposal."

"But how did he get Ms. Hilton down here?" Webb asked.

Rolf snorted and sneezed, pawing at his snout.

"Here," Erin said. "It's the same place he got bothered last time."

She knelt down and sniffed the ground herself, to Rolf's puzzlement and Vic's amusement. The scent of bleach was very faint, but she still caught a little whiff of it.

She stood up and looked around. They were standing on a big concrete slab, fairly fresh, surrounded by many identical slabs.

"So where's the body?" Vic asked.

"Under this," Erin said, tapping the concrete with her foot.

"We can't dig up the whole foundation," Webb said. "The judge would never let that happen. The company could sue the city, even if we found a body."

Erin froze. She'd seen something. "We don't have to dig up the whole thing," she said. "I know where the body is."

"Enlighten us," Webb said.

"Get Ledbetter in here," she said. "He needs to see this."

Vic left and returned with the foreman. Erin pointed to the concrete underfoot.

"Some of this was already poured when we checked this location," she said. "According to you, the site had been shut down for a while. Is that correct?"

"Yeah," Ledbetter said. "There wasn't no money."

"Right," she said. "And concrete sets fast, in less than twenty-four hours, correct?"

"Yeah," he said again. "What's your point, lady? I got the guys coming back here in five minutes, tops."

"Vic, you remember getting pissed off the last time we were here?" Erin asked him.

"I'm always pissed off," he said.

"Point. You stamped your foot this time, remember?"

"Oh, yeah."

"And you were standing right over there." She pointed.

All eyes turned to follow her finger. There, on a neat square of concrete, was the distinct impression of a man's shoe, right down to the tread marks. It wasn't deep, no more than a quarter inch, but it was clear and clean.

"It must've been nearly fully set," she said. "So you hardly sank in, and it held the shape. Go on, Vic. Try the size."

Vic walked over and set his foot in the imprint. It fit perfectly. Wordlessly, he lifted his foot to show the tread pattern on the bottom of his shoe. It was an exact match.

"You're standing on Annmarie Hilton," Erin said.

Chapter 16

Judge Ferris was an old man. Erin didn't know exactly how old, but he had to be in his eighties. He still had a full head of hair, though it had long ago turned pure white. His eyes were set in an incredible topography of wrinkles, but those eyes were as keen and bright as they day he'd graduated law school. He turned the full force of his eyes on Erin as she walked into his office, Rolf at her side and Vic a step behind. Webb had borrowed Vic's car to drive back to the Eightball while Erin and Vic went to see the Judge.

"Hello, young lady," Ferris said. "I'm perfectly charmed to receive your visit this lovely day. Please forgive me for not rising to greet you, but my knee has been giving me grief. The doctors say they replaced it with titanium, but I could swear on a stack of Bibles I still feel pain in the bones. Would you care to take a glass of bourbon with me?"

Erin smiled. She'd always liked Ferris. He'd been old school before the old school had been built. "Sorry, Your Honor. I'm working."

"A pity," Ferris said. "I've considered tucking a bottle of Kentucky's best behind the bench. But my assistant seems to think it would send the wrong message. It's enough to make one wonder why we ever repealed Prohibition."

"You don't need to tell me," she said. "I live over a bar."

"Charming!" Ferris said. "And no doubt you'd rather be there than nattering to an old codger like me. To what do I owe the pleasure?"

"We need a court order to dig up a body," Erin said.

"Is this body legally interred?" the Judge asked.

"No. It's a murder victim. She's buried on a construction site in Manhattan."

Ferris nodded. "That should present no serious difficulties. How do you know the body is there?"

Erin explained their line of reasoning. While she talked, Rolf sat beside her and stared up at her. Vic read the bindings on the Judge's shelf of law books. When she'd finished, Ferris frowned.

"This is a little less cut-and-dried than usual, Detective," he said. "You do have some evidence, but it's largely circumstantial."

Erin opened her mouth to protest. The Judge held up a hand to stop her.

"I'll sign the warrant," he said. "However, you need to understand what happens next. The property owners have no legal recourse for damages incurred, so they're likely to be very upset."

"That bothers us," Vic said. "When people get upset with us. It hurts our feelings. Sometimes I feel bad for at least an hour afterward."

"This isn't like digging up someone's vegetable garden," Ferris said. "If the owners have political clout—and I have reason to believe they do—they can make trouble for the Department. Oh, I'm not worried about myself. I've been sitting on the bench almost half a century. If they manage to shuffle me off, I might thank them. I could use the rest. But it could cause serious difficulties for your careers, Detectives."

"I worry about my career almost as much as I worry about people hurting my feelings," Vic said.

"And there's the added wrinkle of the boy's father owning the lot in question," the Judge said. "In some ways that makes it easier. It's all in the family, so to speak. But you may not have heard the name Lyndon Millhouse. I have. He's a powerful man and a dangerous enemy."

"I'm used to having dangerous enemies," Erin said. "And I get the feeling if I put away his son for murder, he's not going to be my biggest fan no matter what."

"In that case, I'm happy to oblige such an attractive young lady," Ferris said. Coming out of any other man's mouth, it would've sounded like sexual harassment to Erin, but Ferris somehow made it into a compliment. Maybe, she thought, it was because the last time he'd actually been physically interested in a woman, color TV had been a newfangled thing.

"Thank you, Your Honor," was the most diplomatic thing she could think of to say.

*   *   *

"We'll need to get the DDC involved," Vic said once they were outside the Judge's office.

"The who?" Erin asked.

"Department of Design and Construction," he explained. "They're the guys who do all the big city-improvement projects."

"All we need is a backhoe and a couple of guys who know how to use it," she said.

"And the DDC can get those guys."

"Can they do it fast enough?" she asked. "We're on a tight schedule."

"We just need to go through the right channels," he said. "I'll find the right bureaucrat and twist his arm."

"But where is this damn department?"

"That's the beauty of it," he said, grinning. "They're in the Dinkins Building just down the street. We can be there in ten minutes. Drop me at the front door. I'll take care of business and catch the subway back to the Eightball."

"How come you know so much about construction red tape?" she asked.

"A guy I knew in my old precinct used to be an undercover, busting up construction rackets," he said. "That guy had some stories. This isn't the first body that ended up part of New York's architecture."

Erin accordingly deposited Vic for his bout with New York's bureaucracy and made her way south. She and Rolf arrived at the Eightball in time for lunch, which she grabbed from a Chinese takeout place down the block. Then, fortified with chicken chow mein, she went upstairs.

"Got the warrant, sir," she announced, brandishing the piece of paper with Ferris's signature. Then she paused. Captain Holliday was standing at Webb's desk. Both men looked serious.

"Thank you, O'Reilly," Webb said. "Let's just hope we get a chance to use it."

"What are you talking about?" she asked. "Vic's getting the excavating equipment right now. We've got Millhouse!"

"He exercised his right to legal counsel right after we left to go chasing Hilton's phone," Webb said. "Millhouse is down in Interrogation Room One with his lawyer right now. And his dad's on the way. The kid's retracted his confession."

"So what?" Erin demanded. "I said we've got the warrant. We don't need the confession if we can tie him to the body."

"Well, why don't we go talk to him together?" Webb suggested. "You can tell him that. Your dog can hold the fort up here."

Erin was nervous. Holliday's supervision at an interrogation was unusual enough, and she was still smarting from her previous encounter with the Captain. The thought crossed her mind that misconduct allegations could poison this case. She wished she hadn't thought of that. The Captain peeled off into the observation room, leaving Webb and Erin to go into the interrogation room.

Millhouse's lawyer was wearing a suit that probably cost more than Erin's whole wardrobe. He was a big-shouldered man who looked more like a football linebacker than an attorney, but his attitude was calm and competent. And for the first time since she'd laid eyes on the kid, Chris Millhouse wasn't smiling.

"My client wishes to offer an apology to the Department," the lawyer said, launching immediately into action. "He was attending a fraternity party at his university on the night the alleged crime occurred. His recollections are limited, as he experienced a partial blackout, but he believes someone illicitly slipped him a hallucinogenic substance, causing a vivid, lucid dream state in which he genuinely believed he had committed a terrible crime. However, he now recognizes this hallucination for what it was. Obviously, he wishes to retract his spurious confession."

"That's nice," Erin said. "What about the fake text sent from the victim's phone?" With Vic out of the room, someone had to play bad cop, and she was through being nice to this creep.

"There is no victim, Detective," the lawyer said.

"Annmarie Hilton," Erin said. "Your client's psychology professor."

"You have her body?" the lawyer asked.

"We've got her phone and her finger," she said grimly. "And we're about to get the rest of her."

"Her finger?" the lawyer repeated. "So you have physical evidence connecting this finger to my client?"

"Our investigation is ongoing," Webb said quietly.

"Yes, I've heard about your so-called investigation," the lawyer said. "Intimidation and assault of university students. Wildly irresponsible accusations. A complete absence of proof. I demand that you release my client immediately upon his own recognizance. Should you manage to locate, or more likely manufacture, evidence at some point in the future, he will be easy to locate."

"Unless Daddy's dollars pay for a flight to some non-extradition country just like they paid for you," Erin said through clenched teeth.

"More baseless accusations," the lawyer said, unperturbed. "Either charge my client or release him."

"We're not legally obligated to do either until nine o'clock tomorrow morning," Webb said. "Now, is there anything else you'd like to say?"

"It seemed so real," Millhouse said. "But now I know it wasn't. I made the whole thing up. That must be why the woman in my dream looked like my professor. I really am sorry, Detectives, for all the trouble I've put you through. I promise it won't happen again."

He looked wide-eyed and sincere. If Erin hadn't seen Millhouse's smug, creepy stare and heard the things that had come out of his mouth in earlier conversations, she might have been inclined to believe him. She suppressed a shudder.

"You're going back in your cell," she said. "And we're going to dig up your dead professor. Until we do, we're done talking."

* * *

Erin escorted Millhouse to his holding cell. She really wanted to say something to him, to tell him she hadn't fallen for his bullshit and he wasn't fooling anybody. But she also knew he was still playing his game, even if they had him worried, and he'd willfully misconstrue anything she said. He might even accuse her of violating his right to legal counsel, claim she'd asked him questions without his lawyer, or spin some other story. So she kept her face expressionless and her mouth shut.

"I'm going to miss you, Detective," Millhouse said as she guided him into the cell. "It's been a very interesting experience, seeing how the police conduct an investigation. I'll remember it for future reference."

Erin managed not to grimace. She maintained her stoic demeanor. But then, once the cell door was locked and she'd unfastened his handcuffs, she stepped back from the bars, looked him in the eye, and smiled.

"Detective," he said. "This is really pitiful, you know? The silent treatment? A little juvenile, don't you think?"

She gave him nothing. Instead, she turned and walked away.

"Detective!" he called after her. She kept walking. Only after the security door to Holding clicked shut behind her did she let out the breath she'd been holding. Her shoulders ached. She hadn't even known how tense he'd made her.

She found Webb and Holliday in the observation room. Holliday was stroking his mustache. It reminded Erin of the way Marlon Brando petted the cat in the opening scene of *The Godfather*.

"What did you think, sir?" she asked the Captain.

"I think we won't find any trace of hallucinogens in his bloodstream," Holliday said. "Of course, it's been long enough after the fact that they might have metabolized normally. Which he would know. I think you've got a smart, confident, cunning, and very dangerous young man locked up, and I think we should use all legal means to ensure he stays that way."

"So you don't buy his story?"

"I don't imagine you've ever been to Shawangunk, Detective?" Holliday replied.

"No, sir."

"I have," the Captain said. "They've got David Berkowitz there. I've met him."

"Son of Sam?" Erin said. She, like every New York cop, knew about the infamous serial killer who'd killed six people and injured several more back in the Seventies. He'd claimed his neighbor's dog had told him to commit the murders, but had changed his story over the years.

"The same," Holliday said. "Your suspect reminds me of him."

"How so?" Webb asked.

"Some criminals enjoy celebrity," Holliday said. "Al Capone, for instance. Berkowitz liked being famous. He thought the whole thing was a lot of fun. And he enjoyed messing with the police, the psychologists, everybody who tried to understand him. They were doing serious work, he was just playing around. If your guy hits the street, he'll kill again. Not because he has to, but because he wants to."

"My thoughts exactly, sir," Erin said.

"I also think we're going to have a lot of trouble digging up that lot," Holliday said.

"Not with the earth-moving equipment," Webb said. "I just heard from Neshenko. He's got an excavator and a work crew on the way, though Lord only knows what he had to do to get it so fast."

"Don't ask," Holliday said dryly. "That way I can truthfully tell the PC I don't know anything about it. No, the problem is Millhouse's lawyers."

"That no-neck we just talked to can't stop a search warrant," Erin said. "It's completely legal, obtained through proper channels."

"I'm talking about the elder Millhouse. Lyndon Millhouse. He's arguing for an injunction. It won't hold up in court, but it doesn't have to. All it has to do is stall us for less than a day. Then his kid gets out of jail."

"And goes somewhere warm and sunny," Erin added. "I bet he's already got the plane on standby."

Holliday nodded. "What else have we got?"

"The victim's index finger," Erin said. "And her phone."

"Does that do us any good?" Holliday asked.

"We can unlock the phone with the fingerprint," Erin said. "And that's what the killer did, too. He sent a fake suicide e-mail to the victim's brother."

She paused as a thought struck her. "We need to look at that phone," she said. "Millhouse is too smart to have done anything really stupid with it, like log into his own social media accounts, but maybe Annmarie has something buried in her communications. She was targeted. I want to know why. She knew him."

"Go to it, Detective," Holliday said. "You've got a little less than twenty hours to get enough for the DA to charge him."

Chapter 17

"This isn't the weirdest thing I've ever done," Erin said. She held the severed finger in one gloved hand, the phone in the other. "But it's up there."

"Work major cases long enough and that won't even crack the top twenty," Webb said. "You should've seen some of the things we saw in the LAPD."

Erin swiped the finger to unlock the phone. She already had the device plugged into her computer. As soon as the screen lit up, she started downloading the phone's contents. It took a couple of minutes, during which she returned the finger to its evidence bag and set it aside.

Once the download finished, she started going through the files. The days of simple telephone records were long gone. Now she had e-mails, photographs, memos, calendars, and text messages as well as voicemails and call records. She cloned the data and sent Webb a copy. Then they got down to business.

Working against a deadline was tough, no matter what you were doing, but Erin would far rather have been racing a ticking time bomb or running down a fleeing suspect than sitting at a desk, staring at a computer screen. After the first couple of hours, her eyeballs felt like they were drying out. Her headache returned in full force, without even the consolation of having gotten drunk beforehand.

"Nothing in her e-mail folder," she finally said, sitting back and rubbing her eyes.

"Call log is clean too," Webb said. "But Millhouse might have scrubbed the folders."

"He wouldn't have kept the phone long," she said. "If there were any communications between them, he would've deleted them before ditching it. But I think he meant the phone to go into the river, along with the finger. So something might be left."

"Agreed," Webb said dryly. "Not much point sending a suicide note if you leave a severed digit lying around. That's the sort of thing a detective might interpret as evidence of foul play."

"There's got to be something here," Erin muttered. She looked at Annmarie's calendar and saw blank spaces. "Calendar's empty, too," she said.

"Maybe she didn't use it," Webb said. "Hell, I don't even know half the things my phone can do."

"Maybe," she replied. "No disrespect, sir, but Annmarie Hilton was younger than you. And she put all kinds of apps on this thing. Let me just check."

Erin scrolled back to the previous month's calendar. Sure enough, it was packed with class schedules, meetings, appointments, yoga class, and dinners. The woman's whole life was neatly laid out day by day.

"This month's been wiped," she announced.

"Which means there was something on it the killer didn't want us to see," Webb said. "We need one of our forensic techs."

A few minutes later they had one of the Eightball's technical specialists in the office. A heavyset officer with glasses and a soft, gentle voice, he examined the phone. With one more use of

Annmarie's finger, and a grimace of distaste, he logged in and examined the device.

"I should be able to retrieve the deleted data," he said. "It might take a couple of hours."

"Then get started," Webb said.

The technician had just gone back to his lair, which Erin imagined as a subterranean cinderblock room packed with computer equipment and unhealthy snack food, when Sergeant Malcolm called up from the front desk.

"Got some guys here to see you," he said.

"What do they want?" Erin asked.

"They want that kid you've got in Holding. Millhouse. There's three of them out here. The one in the middle, the one in the really nice suit, says he's Millhouse's dad."

"Fantastic," Erin said, loading the word with as much sarcasm as it could carry. "Okay, send them up."

"Company?" Webb asked.

"Millhouse Senior," she said. "And his lawyers, most likely."

Webb stood up and stepped away from his desk.

"Where are you going, sir?" Erin demanded. "You're not leaving me to deal with the lawyers alone, are you?"

"Of course not. What kind of bastard do you think I am? I'm calling backup." He walked to Holliday's door, knocked, and stepped inside. A moment later he stuck his head out.

"We'll do it in here," he said. "With the Captain."

The elevator doors slid back to reveal three men, obviously lawyers or executives of some sort. The one in the middle definitely bore a visual resemblance to Chris Millhouse. He was older, grayer, and a little heavier, but he had the same sleekly handsome face and the same dark, disquieting eyes.

Erin stepped forward. Rolf was up on his paws, staring at the newcomers. Though no one had spoken yet, and nobody had made any aggressive move, the K-9's hackles rose.

"Sir," she said. "I'm Detective Erin O'Reilly. What can I do—"

"Are you in charge?" the man in the middle interrupted.

"I'm her commanding officer, Lieutenant Webb," Webb said.

"Are *you* in charge?"

"No, sir. That would be the precinct captain."

"Then why am I talking to some middle-management pencil-pusher?" the man snapped.

"If you'll just follow me, please," Webb said blandly.

The man blew past Erin as if she wasn't even there. He spared Webb only marginally more attention.

"Good thing Vic's not here," Erin said in a very low undertone to Webb as the strangers trooped into Holliday's office. Erin thought about leaving Rolf outside; the Captain's office was small and would be cramped even without ninety extra pounds of fur and teeth. But she decided to bring him anyway. This seemed like the sort of meeting where a little extra intimidation might not be a bad thing. She closed the door behind them and stood in front of it, Rolf beside her.

The Captain was already on his feet, hand extended. "Good afternoon, sir," he said. "I'm Fenton Holliday, Captain of Precinct 8. Am I correct in assuming you are Lyndon Millhouse?"

"That's right," Millhouse said. He stared at Holliday's hand with the look most people reserved for roadkill and dogshit. "Do you know where I was this morning, Mr. Holliday?"

"*Captain* Holliday," the Captain said with slight emphasis. Erin knew Holliday to be a fair-minded, decent man, but she also knew he was a tough former street cop and not a man to be taken lightly. Her guts still churned a little from the quiet chewing-out he'd given her.

"I was in Paris," Millhouse said. "That's Paris, France. Not Paris, Arkansas; not Paris, Kentucky; and definitely not the Podunk unincorporated wide spot in the road that goes by Paris, Michigan. I was in Paris for a hundred-million-dollar telecommunications deal. I had to fly back to New York on extremely short notice, *commercial air. Business class.*"

"I understand that must have been a significant inconvenience for a man of your means," Holliday said with icy diplomacy, demonstrating why he was a Captain and Erin probably never would be. "Now that you're here, it would be a shame to waste any more of your valuable time. How may I help you?"

"You can stop holding my son hostage," Millhouse said.

"Your son is not a hostage," Holliday said. "He is being held on the basis of a voluntary and unsolicited confession of first-degree murder."

"Nonsense," Millhouse said. "He did no such thing."

"He definitely confessed to murder," Webb said. "I was there. I saw him and heard him, as did two other detectives. He made a sworn statement."

"Then why has he not been charged?" the man on Millhouse's right, whom Erin mentally labeled Lawyer #1, demanded.

"Legally, the NYPD has forty-eight hours in which we can hold a suspect before bringing charges," Holliday said. "We are collecting additional evidence as we speak."

"Meaning you don't have any now!" Millhouse snapped. "You can't hold a kid just based on something he said!"

"Corpus Delicti," said the man on Millhouse's left, Lawyer #2. "You cannot charge on the basis of confession alone. And even if you did, my client's son would be within his Constitutional rights to claim Fifth Amendment protection at whatever farce of a trial you managed to scrape together."

"Several points," Holliday said. His voice was quiet but his tones were clipped, cold, and formal, his diction perfect. "Firstly, Christopher Millhouse is not a kid. He is nineteen years old, an adult in the eyes of the law. Secondly, the New York Police Department does not put suspects on trial; that is the purview of the Manhattan District Attorney. Thirdly, Mr. Millhouse was the one to claim we have no evidence. That is factually incorrect."

"Let's see the evidence, then!" Millhouse said.

"Evidence will be presented to the grand jury, in accordance with the law," Holliday replied. "I am under no obligation to present it to you at this time and place, sir. It would be grossly inappropriate."

"Do you know who I am?" Millhouse demanded.

Erin and Webb shared a sidelong, wryly amused glance. There wasn't a cop in the world who hadn't been asked that question, and there wasn't a cop they knew who respected any man who asked it. In their experience, the only men who played that worn-out old card were entitled assholes who thought the rules didn't apply to them.

"You are Lyndon Millhouse," Holliday said, unruffled. "Chief Executive Officer of Wildfyre, Inc., a major telecommunications company. You have a net worth estimated at between seven and eight hundred million dollars. You are a part-time resident of New York City, and are therefore accorded the same courtesy and respect I would grant to any citizen in good standing before the law. Now, do you know who I am?"

"You're a jumped-up security guard who thinks his shit smells like roses because he's got a fancy badge and a corner office," Millhouse said. "And maybe he thinks just because he shifted some rubble at the World Trade Center, it makes him more than a glorified janitor."

Erin blinked. She couldn't possibly have heard him right. She saw Webb's mouth drop open. Webb hadn't been with the NYPD on 9/11; he'd still been serving with the LAPD on the opposite coast. And Erin hadn't graduated college yet. But Holliday had been on active duty. Erin had seen him in full-dress uniform and had seen the gold-bordered black WTC ribbon on his jacket. He'd been there, all right. He'd probably pulled bodies of his fellow cops out of the wreckage. Those weren't just fighting words; what Millhouse had said was a declaration of war.

Holliday's face didn't so much as twitch. "I understand you're upset, sir," he said. "And I understand we've only just met, so you can't be expected to know me. You probably haven't had much contact with law-enforcement personnel, so I'll give you a pass on your lack of manners. Actually, I should thank you. You're helping me understand the situation much better."

"And what situation is that?" Millhouse sneered.

"Sir," Lawyer #1 said. "You really should let us do the talking."

"The situation in which your son now finds himself," Holliday said. "I'd been wondering why he might have thought he could commit a major felony, brag about it to the NYPD, and expect nothing to come of it. Now, seeing the role model he had growing up, and the complete absence of consequences for his actions he must have enjoyed, it's much clearer. Thank you for demonstrating the way you've contributed to this."

"You little rat-faced bastard," Millhouse said. "Don't you dare tell me how I should've raised my boy."

"This isn't a moral question, Mr. Millhouse," Holliday said. "It's simply a matter of actions and consequences. The NYPD deals in the law, not in morality."

"I don't think this meeting is being productive, sir," Lawyer #2 said, glancing uneasily at Lawyer #1. "Maybe we should—"

"You think you can lock up my boy and dig up my property?" Millhouse said, riding right over his lawyer. "And you talk about consequences? I'm going to burn you so bad they'll use your balls for briquettes! You bring your damn shovels and try to shut down my building site? It's harassment! Do you have any idea how hard it was to put together the financing for that building? Dealing with the damn construction union? They're going to keep working, damn it! And if you want whatever's under the foundations, you can damn well wait until the building falls down!"

Erin had a sudden thought. She shot Webb a meaningful look.

"Sir," she said when Millhouse paused for breath, "I need to make a phone call. It's urgent."

"You're dismissed, Detective," Holliday said. He returned his attention to Millhouse, who had reloaded his arsenal of words and was getting ready to unleash another volley. His face remained carefully composed behind the protective shield of his mustache. "You were saying, sir?"

Erin and Rolf made their escape. The door muffled Millhouse's angry ranting. Erin scooted across the room and hauled out her phone.

"Yes, darling?" Carlyle said, picking up on the second ring.

"I need to talk to Corky," she said. "Do you have a phone number?"

"Aye," he said. "Everything all right?"

"Yeah. This isn't about that thing. It's something else."

"Very well. The lad's just gotten a new burner. Here's the number."

Erin jotted it down on her notepad. "Thanks! See you tonight."

"I'll look forward to it."

Then she called the new number, wondering whether Corky would even pick up. He didn't seem the most reliable communicator. The phone rang once, twice, three times, four. She sighed and got ready to try it again.

"If you're selling something, I'm not buying, unless you're a lovely lass," Corky said by way of greeting.

"I am," Erin said. "But I don't think you want any of what I've got for you."

There was the briefest pause. Then he said, "Erin, love! What a surprise! Don't tell me Cars broke it off with you? I'll never forgive him, but I'll gladly give you a shoulder to cry on. Or other parts of me, come to that. My entire physiology is at your disposal."

"I'll remember that," she said, glad they were back to their easy banter. Things had been pretty strained between them ever since Michelle's kidnapping and the events of the previous day. "Who do you know in the Manhattan construction unions?"

"Practically everybody, love, from the union president right on down."

"Do you know a guy called Moe Ledbetter?"

"Know him? Love, I got drunk with him at his son's graduation party last year! Fine lad. Best foreman money can buy."

"Great!" Erin had been hoping, but hadn't been sure this would pan out. Corky was extremely well connected with both the Teamsters and most of the other big New York labor unions. He had friends everywhere.

"What's poor Moe done to earn your attention?" Corky asked. "He's no more crooked than most."

"Nothing," she said. "But he's sitting on something important. How hard do you think it'd be to arrange a labor slowdown on a site he's working?"

"I'll make some calls, love. What's the game?"

"We need to dig up a body," she said. "And Moe and his guys are trying to pour more concrete on top of it."

"Does he know about the body in question?"

"Yeah, but don't worry, he didn't put it there. I promise he won't get in any trouble over this."

"You talk about trouble?" he said. "Nod's as good as a wink, love. Give me a few shakes and I'll cause more trouble than you can imagine. Anything else you can tell me about this place we're shutting down?"

She tried to remember. "It's got a bunch of nasty chemical shit. Some of it spilled on the ground. Maybe some sort of health-code violation?"

He laughed, and Erin could practically see the mischief dancing in his eyes. "Perfect," he said. "I've just the thing. I know lad to handle this."

Erin hung up and considered her options. From behind Holliday's door came Lyndon Millhouse's angry tones. That man sure loved the sound of his own voice. Every now and then, Holliday or Webb would interject something, but Millhouse was doing ninety percent of the talking. Erin wondered what he'd bothered bringing his lawyers along for.

She decided to try tech support. It took a minute for her to find their phone extension; she wasn't in the habit of calling them. But she got through to the same soft-spoken technician that had been up in Major Crimes.

"Got anything off that phone yet?" she asked.

"Well, yes, a little. I've recovered the calendar."

"Great. Send me that."

"But I'm not done with the full retrieval yet. If you can give me a couple of hours, like I asked—"

"Send it. Now."

"Uh... okay."

A few moments later, Annmarie Hilton's monthly schedule for September was in front of Erin's face on her computer screen. Sixty seconds after that, she was knocking on Holliday's door, printout in hand. Rolf, panting with excitement, was right beside her.

"Just a moment, sir," Holliday said, cutting Millhouse off mid-sentence. "As you recently reminded me, I'm on the public payroll and currently on the clock, so I do have work to do. Come in, Detective."

Erin entered. Millhouse was obviously furious. Webb looked tired and in need of tobacco. Holliday was as calm and collected as before, but Erin thought he looked slightly more frayed around the edges.

"Welcome back, Detective," Holliday said. "What've you got there?"

"Annmarie Hilton's planner," she said triumphantly. "Here."

Holliday plucked it out of her hand and scanned it. "Interesting," he said. "Mr. Millhouse, it seems the missing Ms. Hilton had scheduled a meeting at O'Hara's Pub for ten-thirty on the night of her disappearance."

"So?" Millhouse said.

"O'Hara's is less than a block from your construction site," Erin said.

"So?" Millhouse said again. "She went to a bar. What does that prove?"

Holliday turned the paper around and pointed with his index finger. The line he indicated read: "10:30, C. Millhouse, O'Hara's."

"She was meeting with our confessed killer, only a few yards from the site our warrant empowers us to search," Holliday said. "We're going to dig up that foundation, Mr. Millhouse, no matter what you do, and we'll find what's buried there."

"Not in the next twenty-four hours, you won't," Millhouse said, getting himself under control. "I'll call in every favor I've got."

"What are you so eager to hide?" Erin asked quietly.

Lawyer #1 put out a hand. "Sir, please don't engage," he said.

Millhouse shook the hand off. "I don't have to explain myself to you," he said. "You're nothing."

"You already knew about Chris," she said, looking into his eyes. "You've known what he was for a long time. Years, I imagine. What tipped you off? Usually guys like him start small. Animals. Did he have a pet as a boy? What happened to it?"

Millhouse stared at her. "Who told you that?" he demanded. "Who've you been talking to?"

"You weren't home much," she went on. "Chris had a nanny, didn't he? Did she tell you the truth about him, or did she try to hide it from you?"

"We're done here," Lawyer #2 said, trying to salvage the situation. "You can contact our office with any further questions."

"We're done when I say we're done," Millhouse said. "Once I've explained something to this little bitch. Listen, you think you're hot stuff in those tight pants with that shiny gold badge, but you don't know a damn thing about me. Here's the lowdown, sweetie. It doesn't matter what my boy's done. It doesn't matter what you think he is. Because he's mine. He's my boy and I'm going to take care of him. You get me? No matter what it takes. You can get all the court orders you want. But you don't come onto my property to dig up dirt on my boy. Those men are still working on my tower, and they'll keep working until I tell them to stop. And do you know why? Because I've got the money and you've got nothing. So yeah, now we're done here. For the moment. But I won't forget this. All of you are going to regret what you tried to do. I'm walking out of here, and my boy's coming with me, and there's not a damn thing you can do to stop me."

Lawyer #1 paused in the middle of another fruitless attempt to shut his boss up. He pulled out his phone and looked at the screen. He started.

"Sir," he said. "You need to see this."

"Not now," Millhouse said.

"Yes, now," the lawyer insisted.

"Okay, what is it?"

"The crew just walked off the job," the lawyer said. "They put down their tools and walked away. Mr. Ledbetter says his union rep is calling a walkout."

Millhouse's face froze. "They can't do that," he said.

Holliday and Webb both looked at Erin. She maintained a rigid poker face. There'd be a time for gloating, pretty soon now, but not quite yet.

"The city excavation crew is moving onto the site right now, sir," Lawyer #1 said.

"Well, stop them!" Millhouse snapped.

"We're filing an injunction," the lawyer said. "But it'll take a little more time. And I really should be at the courthouse."

"Then what the hell are you doing standing around here?" Millhouse exploded.

"Sir, you requested we accompany you," Lawyer #2 said.

"Shut up! Follow me!" Millhouse stormed out of the office, trailed by his underlings. He jabbed the elevator call button several times. When the doors didn't immediately open, he rushed down the stairs. The three police officers and one dog emerged from Holliday's office and watched them go. Holliday cocked an eyebrow at Erin.

"Labor union walkout?" he said.

She shrugged. "It's important to maintain good relations with contractors," she said. "Otherwise all kinds of things can go wrong."

"Quite a coincidence, the timing of that," Holliday said.

"I don't think O'Reilly believes in coincidence, sir," Webb said.

"Or the Tooth Fairy," Erin said. "But who knows? I found quarters under my pillow when I was a kid. That's circumstantial, but it's evidence."

Webb's phone buzzed. He hauled it out and swiped the screen.

"Webb," he said. "Neshenko? Yes, we just heard about that here. Yes, it's great news, but your guys need to work fast. A very angry executive and his pack of lawyers are on their way right now. No, you're not allowed to shoot them. No, the Taser is also not an option. What's that? Sorry, I didn't hear you clearly. We must have a bad connection. Webb out."

He hung up and turned his attention back to Erin and Holliday. "They're digging," he reported. "Neshenko will do everything he legally can to keep Millhouse away from the site."

"By that, do you mean—" Erin began.

"Everything he legally can," Webb repeated in a flat deadpan.

"I'd better get down there," she said. "They may still need Rolf's nose."

"Good luck, Detective," Holliday said. "And well done."

"You too, sir."

"Me?" Holliday looked surprised. "What did I do?"

"You let that bastard bounce off you, sir. After some of the things he said, I wanted to throw him out your window."

Holliday rubbed his mustache. "That's the Job, Detective. Do your work well enough and you may get promoted high enough to discover that for yourself."

"I like working cases, sir. I'll leave the politics to guys like you."

"Did you just call me a politician, O'Reilly?" Holliday asked.

"Not technically, sir."

"I'm glad to hear it. I'd hate to lose your good opinion." Then Holliday winked.

Chapter 18

A proverb about traffic, particularly New York traffic, held that the less time you had to get somewhere, the worse the traffic would be. Erin hit a traffic jam four blocks from the construction site. It was hard gridlock, no movement at all. The lights and sirens would be pointless; even if the other cars wanted to get out of her way, there was nowhere for them to go.

Erin went through the accelerated phases of grieving from denial through anger, skipped the bargaining stage, and accepted the situation. She worked the Charger sideways into a police spot and got out, unloading Rolf.

"Looks like we're walking it, kiddo," she told him.

Rolf wagged his tail. He loved walks. This was a great plan.

They jogged along the sidewalk, passing stalled cars by the dozen. The blare of horns blended into a chaotic background harmony. Erin wondered what had happened. A car accident, probably. It wasn't uncommon for a single fender-bender to make traffic back up halfway down the island; it was just inconvenient for her right now. Though it might be even worse for Lyndon Millhouse. He'd have to get to the courthouse before going to the construction site, so she had a head start that would only get bigger in a foot chase. Millhouse didn't look like he worked out as often as she did.

From a block away, Erin could see the flashing police lights. It looked like whatever had happened was right next to her destination. She sped up. A suspicion was growing in her paranoid detective's mind.

As she threaded her way across the last cross-street, she slowed to a walk. She wasn't sure whether to laugh or bury her face in her hands. The police cars on scene weren't responding to an accident; they were part of the accident. Front and center was Vic's Taurus, its rear fender crumpled. It had T-boned an NYPD Patrol car, having backed straight into it. The blue-and-white had been jammed against a lamp post in the intersection and, together with the Taurus, blocked the traffic in all directions.

Vic was standing in the middle of the intersection, talking to a couple of uniforms. Nobody appeared to be working on clearing the accident, though several more cops were standing around the perimeter. Behind them, on the construction site, a backhoe was chugging away, clawing at the concrete. A couple of big, burly guys with jackhammers were punching holes in the foundation, loosening it for the big earth-mover.

"Vic, what did you do?" Erin asked.

"Oh, hey, Erin," Vic said. He wasn't particularly upset. If anything, he seemed cheerful. "Craziest thing. I guess I just forgot to do a mirror check. Backed right into Watson here. Screwed up his ride."

Patrolman Watson didn't look as chipper as Vic. He scowled. "And Neshenko the demolition derby detective won't let us clear the street," he said. "Transportation Bureau's gonna chew out my Captain, Captain's gonna yell at my Lieutenant, who's gonna yell at my Sergeant, and what am I supposed to tell him when he yells at me?"

"Tell him it was my fault," Vic said, unconcerned.

"Just explain to me how this is serving the public trust," Watson growled. "Why can't we clear this mess around the corner, at least? Nobody can move on either street!"

"Important Major Crimes business," Vic said. "Don't worry. We'll get your car moved as soon as we finish digging out that chunk of concrete over there."

"What's that got to do with anything?" Watson was at least as confused as he was exasperated.

"Above your pay grade, Patrolman," Vic said.

"Can I have a word, Detective?" Erin asked, taking Vic's arm and tugging him away.

"I'll be right back," Vic told Watson. "Don't go anywhere."

"It'd be pretty goddamn hard for me to go anywhere, don't you think?" Watson shouted after him.

"Vic," Erin said more quietly, their voices screened by the clatter of the jackhammers. "What exactly happened?"

"Just what it looks like," he said. "Car accident."

"You can fool them, but you can't fool me," she said. "You're a better driver than that."

"You don't believe I backed into that squad car?"

"No, I absolutely believe that. What I don't believe is that it was an accident."

"Well, as I recall, I was given a direct order to slow down access to this site by all legal means," Vic said. "Got the idea from Zofia, from a traffic jam Janovich caused that one time he rammed his suspect into a stoplight."

"What's legal about ramming an NYPD squad car?" she hissed, trying to keep her voice down and almost succeeding.

"I think it's about as legal as using your Mob contacts with the construction union to orchestrate a work slowdown," Vic replied, pitching his own voice so low she could barely hear him. But he grinned as he said it.

"How'd you know?" she replied.

"Wasn't hard to figure out. I was standing right next to that chump Ledbetter when he got the call from his rep. It was Corcoran, wasn't it? He's the O'Malleys' union guy."

"You know, Vic, you look like such a musclebound thug, I sometimes forget what a good detective you are," she said.

"That's why I like you, Erin. Even your compliments sound like insults."

"There's some guy in a suit here, too. Says he's from the DEC or some such agency."

"What does he want?"

"You can ask him. He's right over there." Vic pointed with his thumb.

"How's the digging going?"

"Okay. They should have that block of concrete out in the next ten or fifteen minutes. Then we'll know if your hunch was right. It'd better be."

"Tell me about it." Erin shook her head. "Between the excessive force complaint, pissing off a multi-millionaire along with the Columbia campus police, and now causing a major traffic jam in downtown Manhattan, if we don't have a body to show for it, we're all screwed. What if we got it wrong?"

"Don't worry," Vic said. "It's the right place. The footprint was a perfect match. I looked at my shoe. There's traces of concrete in the treads. Hey, think about it. We catch killers by matching footprints all the time."

"Yeah," she said. "But it's usually the killer's footprint, not the detective's."

"That's a first," he agreed. "One for the textbooks."

As Erin approached the site, she saw the suit Vic had indicated. He looked like a dry, humorless little man in an off-the-rack business suit and rimless eyeglasses. He was taking notes on a clipboard.

"Excuse me, sir?" Erin said.

"Yes, ma'am?" he said.

"Detective O'Reilly, NYPD," she said, flashing her shield.

"Vernon Riefko, DEC," the little man replied.

"I'm sorry, what's the DEC?" she asked.

"Department of Environmental Conservation," he explained. "We got a report of potential environmental contaminants being illegally dumped at this location. This construction site is shut down pending further investigation."

"Who called in the complaint?"

"Construction union," he replied. "The representative expressed urgent concerns regarding the wellbeing of their workers."

"You guys moved fast," she said, thinking, *God bless you, James Corcoran.*

"Hmm, yes," Riefko said. "Usually this sort of personal site visit takes two to four weeks to arrange, but my office was able to move my schedule around to make it possible."

Erin wondered how Corky had managed that, and immediately decided not to ask. It had probably involved bribery of city officials, and was therefore a crime.

"Thank you for your prompt action," was what she said, giving him a friendly nod. "I hope this digging won't present a problem."

"Hmm, I'd rather they didn't," Riefko said. "But my brief only extends as far as the construction workers contracted to work this location. It does not include other city employees engaged in police business."

Erin left him to take his notes and rejoined Vic. They watched the excavation for a few minutes, trying to ignore the cacophony of angry horns. Then one of the workmen waved his arms at the backhoe operator. The driver carefully worked the backhoe's arm, drawing a broken chunk of foundation out at an angle. The men stepped back.

"Moment of truth," Vic said.

Erin, Vic, and Rolf approached the hole. They peered into it. Erin's heart fell. All she saw was dirt.

"Well, shit," Vic said.

"That's impossible," Erin said. "It's got to be here."

One of the jackhammer guys came over. To Erin's surprise, he looked familiar. It took her a second to remember that she'd seen him at the Barley Corner a couple of times.

"Ma'am," he said, touching the brim of his hard hat. "What's the problem?"

"There's supposed to be a dead body there," she said.

"That's not the only thing there's supposed to be," he said.

"What do you mean?" she asked.

He shrugged. "Looks like the guys who poured this forgot to add the rebar. There's no reinforcing bars, just concrete."

"Meaning what?" Vic asked.

"This wasn't poured by professionals," he said.

Erin turned to Rolf. The K-9 looked up at her and cocked his head.

"Rolf, *such!*" she ordered.

Rolf sniffed the air. Then, with no hesitation whatsoever, he jumped into the hole. He started scratching at the dirt and whining, his tail lashing eagerly.

"Shovels!" Vic called. "Somebody find some shovels!"

Only a couple of guys could fit in the hole. Rolf leaped and scrambled out at Erin's command. He spent an enjoyable few minutes gnawing on his chew-toy while two men with shovels dug, careful not to stab the spades too deeply for fear of damaging evidence. Erin and Vic watched and waited.

"She's there," Erin said.

"You're sure?" Vic said.

"Rolf's sure," she said. "That's good enough for me."

"Stop!" a man shouted.

Unsurprised, Erin turned to see Lyndon Millhouse, red-faced, sweaty, and puffing. Lawyer #2 was trailing him, very out of breath. Millhouse held up a piece of paper.

"This is an injunction!" he gasped out. "Signed by a New York judge! You are to stop digging at once!"

"Who's the judge?" Vic asked.

"What does it matter?" Millhouse retorted. "It's a legally-binding document!"

"I'm just wondering whose financials to check," Vic said. "In case he got a sudden mysterious infusion of cash."

"What are you implying?" Lawyer #2 had arrived and now entered the conversation.

"I'll need to inspect the document," Vic said. "Make sure it's all legal and above-board."

"You're stalling!" Millhouse said.

Vic took the paper from him and squinted at it. "It's kinda hard to read in this light," he said. "Maybe I should've brought my glasses."

Vic didn't wear glasses. Erin knew this, but Millhouse didn't.

Riefko came over, the DEC bureaucrat drawn by the irresistible rustle of official paperwork. "Excuse me," he said. "Is this pertinent to my inspection?"

"Who's this little dipshit?" Millhouse growled.

"I beg your pardon, sir," Riefko said indignantly. "There's no call for that. I represent the DEC and this site is in violation of several environmental statutes."

"Shut up," Millhouse said. "I'll deal with you in a minute."

Riefko drew himself up to his full height, slightly less than Erin's five-foot six. "You may deal with my office in its official capacity," he said coldly. "But in the meantime, no further construction activity is permitted here."

"What the hell do you call that?" Millhouse demanded, pointing to the excavation crew.

"Official police business," Erin said.

"Which is what this injunction will shut down," Lawyer #2 said.

"What's this word here, Erin?" Vic asked. "I can't quite make it out."

She looked over his shoulder. "Which word?" she asked, playing along.

"Stop this minute!" Millhouse shouted.

"'Pursuant,'" Erin said.

"What's it mean?" Vic asked.

"Following," she translated.

"Oh, right," he said.

"I'll sue you," Millhouse promised. "I'll wreck your pitiful little lives. Both of you!"

"Quiet," Vic said. "I'm trying to read here. You made me lose my place. Now I have to start over."

"While we're discussing things," Riefko said, "I couldn't help but notice the oil leakage from that automobile accident. It appears to be trickling down into the storm drain, and constitutes an illegally-dumped pollutant."

Millhouse looked like he might strangle the DEC bureaucrat on the spot. For the first time, Erin sympathized with the executive just a little.

"Got something!" a workman called from the hole. "God, it's an arm!"

"Excuse me, sir," Erin said. "It sounds like we've found evidence of a crime."

By the time she got to the edge of the hole, the workmen had unearthed most of the left arm of a woman, obviously dead, buried face-down in the dirt. The index finger of the hand was missing.

Erin turned to Millhouse. "Sir, we've got a dead body here," she said. "It appears to be that of Annmarie Hilton, missing and presumed murdered. We've got a finger already in our possession that matches the missing digit. You were saying something about an injunction?"

"Sir," the lawyer said quietly. Erin missed the rest of what the man said to his employer, but caught the words "obstruction of justice."

She turned to Vic. "Better tell Watson he can move his car," she said. "And you might want to do something with your Taurus."

"The Department had better cover the repairs," he said. "That's line-of-duty damage, right there. That car took one for the team."

*   *   *

Chris Millhouse stood in his holding cell, smiling his creepy smile, watching Erin and Vic walk into Holding.

"Okay, jerkoff," Vic said. "You know the drill. Face the wall, hands behind you, through the slot. Time to go."

"My time isn't up until tomorrow morning," Millhouse said, obeying.

"We don't want you here anymore," Erin said. "And we need to hose out the cell to make room for tonight's batch of drunk and disorderly idiots."

Vic snapped the bracelets around Millhouse's wrists. "Okay," he said again. "Now stand back."

Erin opened the cell door. "March," she said.

"Should I call my lawyer?" Millhouse asked. "Or are we skipping the interrogation?"

"We can skip that part," Erin said. "I don't think anybody cares what else you have to say."

"That's too bad," he said. "It's been informative. I think I'm really getting to know you, Detective."

"I doubt it," she said, steering him past the interrogation rooms to the elevator.

Vic stepped around her, giving Millhouse a wide berth, and pushed the "down" button. The doors slid open.

"Is there an intelligence requirement to be a detective?" Millhouse asked.

"Yeah," Vic said. "If you're too smart, you know better than to sign up. Then you end up in Internal Affairs or Public Relations."

"The only reason I asked is that you pushed the wrong button. The lobby is upstairs."

Erin maneuvered him into the elevator to join Vic. Vic hit the button for the garage. The elevator whirred downward.

"Did you push the wrong button, Vic?" Erin asked.

"Let me check. I'm just an idiot detective, what do I know?" He squinted at the buttons. "Nope, that's the one I meant to punch."

"Oh, that's right," Erin said. "We're not going to the lobby, Chris."

She felt the sudden tenseness in his shoulders and got ready for a fight. It would be crazy for a skinny, handcuffed guy to try to overpower Erin, much less her and Vic together, but you never could tell. That was why neither of them was wearing a gun. When you were handling a prisoner, it was best not to have a lethal weapon where he might be tempted to lunge for it.

"Where are we going?" Millhouse asked. He tried to make the question casual, but his voice betrayed him.

The elevator came to a halt. The doors rolled back. There was Lieutenant Webb. Rolf sat beside him, tongue hanging out, looking uncommonly pleased with himself. And behind them was a blue-and-white NYPD prisoner transport van with a pair of uniformed cops standing ready.

"Riker's Island," Erin said. "To await trial. You're being formally charged with the first-degree murder of Annmarie Hilton."

Millhouse couldn't help himself. He braced his feet as well as he could, trying to plant himself in the elevator. But Erin and Vic had handled hundreds of suspects in their careers, most of them bigger, stronger, and more violent. They got him moving again without even breaking a sweat. The uniforms opened the sliding door in the van and helped load him in. They hooked him up to the built-in restraints. Erin and Vic took a seat next to him.

"Don't worry," Vic said. "We'll get you on the road soon enough. We just thought we should have a little chat before you go. And don't worry about your lawyer. You don't have to answer any questions."

"We have everything," Erin said. "Annmarie's body, along with a piece of bloody rebar and a pair of bolt cutters."

"Nice thinking, burying the weapon with the body," Vic added. "As long as we didn't find it, we couldn't match it to you. And you probably wore gloves, but there's still likely to be trace DNA on one or the other."

"The bolt cutters match the cuts to the lock on the construction site and the victim's hand," Erin continued. "We've got her severed finger and her phone. I bet you thought you were being clever, sending that fake suicide message."

"Should've gone a little farther out on the bridge," Vic said. "That park sticks out more than you'd think. You missed the river by a few yards."

"And our technician just finished retrieving the data from her phone," Erin said. "See, it's really hard to permanently delete e-mails, text messages, and other stuff. A good forensic tech can almost always find it.

"Annmarie was worried about you," she went on. "We found an e-mail she sent to your father. She was concerned you were exhibiting classic signs of being a latent serial killer. The papers you'd written for her class, the questions you were asking, all of it was just chock-full of red flags for a trained psychologist."

"Kids are never as good at hiding things as they think they are," Vic said. "I never thought my mom knew the shit I got up to when I was your age. Boy, was I wrong. She knew *everything*."

"We found the e-mail Annmarie sent you," Erin said. "Two weeks before she was killed. The awful thing is, she was trying to help you. She was concerned, and she thought maybe she could divert you before you did anything really bad. You knew better than to send a reply, and you deleted her e-mail when you took her phone, but our guy found it.

"That was when you decided to kill her. See, if she knew what you were, she'd be a danger to you down the road. That's when you had a great idea. You could take care of her and make your first kill at the same time. You'd heard rumors around campus of a computer whiz who was planning the mother of all pranks. He was going to punk the entire city of New York. You pumped his roommate for information and dosed him with his own brand of date-rape drugs so he'd black out the conversation."

"Can't blame you too much for that one," Vic said. "That guy's an asshole. I mean, it's still a felony, but he definitely had it coming."

"Once you knew the time of the power outage, you set a meeting with Annmarie," Erin said. "It might've worried her, but you asked to meet at a pub. There'd be plenty of other people around. It'd be safe enough. But she never made it to the bar."

Erin stared into Millhouse's eyes, looking for something human, some spark of remorse or recognition. She saw only black emptiness, like a city whose power grid had gone down.

"The lights went out right on schedule," she said. "And you were ready. You had everything all set. The hole was already dug, the cement was already there. Who'd think to look for a body buried in concrete when the whole area was covered with it? You knew construction had stalled, but you also knew it was about to resume. It was perfect. Your dad's building would go up on top of Annmarie's grave and nobody would ever know."

Erin needed him to hear this last part. She knew it was the only payback she could give him that might actually get through.

"You could've gotten away with it," she said. "If you hadn't tried to be so damn smart. You couldn't just be quiet and efficient. You had to have an audience, had to play your little game, had to prove you were smarter than we were. Every clue we found was because of something you did, Chris. We didn't beat you. You beat yourself. You know those serial-killer movies you're so fond of? There's one thing they've all got in common. They all get caught. And so did you."

"I'll get out," Millhouse said.

"Maybe," Vic said. "Eventually. I'm betting you get twenty-to-life. So maybe you'll only be thirty-nine or so. But I'm guessing the parole board's going to take one look at you and lock you away again. And I guarantee, if Erin or I are still around, we'll show up for your hearings and make sure they know exactly what you are. I may be kinda dumb, but I've got a long memory for scumbags like you."

"I know people," Millhouse said. "And they're powerful. They'll get me out. You'll see."

"Your dad?" Erin asked. "He'll be lucky if we don't nail him as an accessory. See, the way I see it, Annmarie's e-mail to him was the start of the whole thing, so he had to have said something to you. And with the foundation of his building being used to stash the body... well, just imagine how that looks."

"We might not be able to bring charges," Vic said. "But what do you think Wildfyre's stock price will do when we go public with what we know? I think Daddy's gonna keep his mouth shut and look out for himself."

"That's the thing about psychopaths," Erin said. She stood up. "They don't really believe other people are real. In the end, they're only out for themselves. If your dad's anything like you, and I think he is, he'll throw you under the bus long before he puts himself in any real danger."

Millhouse licked his lips. Suddenly he looked much younger and less sure of himself. "You're wrong," he whispered.

"Am I?" she retorted. "Here's something to ask yourself one of those long nights in maximum security. If you were in his place, and it was your kid, what would you do?"

Erin, Vic, Webb, and Rolf watched the transport van roll up the ramp and out of the garage. Erin scratched Rolf behind the ears. He nudged her hand with his snout.

"That was harsh," Vic said. "But I liked it. You think any of it'll stick?"

"How do I know?" Erin replied. "I'm no psychologist. We'd have to ask Annmarie. But she thought there was hope for him. Otherwise she wouldn't have tried to save him."

"It's not always smart to try to save someone," Webb said thoughtfully. "You try to rescue a drowning man, sometimes he just drags you down with him."

Erin thought of Carlyle, the reluctant criminal who kept going to church, trying to atone for his sins. Then she thought of Corky. Corky loved being a gangster. He laughed at the law and at danger. If not for her and Carlyle, there was no way he'd ever give up the Life. But there was still hope.

"Sometimes," she said. "But you never know."

Chapter 19

"I'm home," Erin announced, jogging up the apartment stairs. Rolf bounded beside her, tongue hanging out. The rest of the workday had been spent logging evidence, writing reports, and swimming through the inevitable ocean of paperwork. But she still felt jazzed. They'd gotten a big win and put away a very dangerous young man. Erin always liked beating the bad guys who thought they were smart. It was like playing a very high-stakes game, knowing the opponent was good, but finding out you were that little bit better.

She found Carlyle in the living room, on the couch. In the chair across from him sat Corky. Both men held shot glasses in their hands.

"Evening, darling," Carlyle said, getting to his feet.

"How's about you, love?" Corky said, following suit and grinning. "I hope I was helpful."

"Corky told me he'd offered you some small assistance," Carlyle said. "But he's been quite cagey as to precisely what he did for you."

"We needed to shut down a construction site for a few hours," she said.

"As it turns out, I know a lad," Corky said. "I hope it was in a good cause?"

"We caught a serial killer," she said. "Well, technically he wasn't one yet. We stopped him at number one."

"Grand," Carlyle said. "That's worth a drink, surely. I've a glass here with your name on it."

"Is that why you're up here?" Erin asked Corky as Carlyle poured her a shot of the good stuff. "To gloat?"

"Perish the thought, love," Corky said. "A gentleman doesn't gloat."

"And just how would you know what a gentleman does?" she shot back.

"I've heard stories," he said. "Nay, I came up to discuss the other situation."

"Oh. Right. I guess I should hear what's happening." Erin sat down on the couch. Carlyle sat next to her. Corky flopped casually back into his chair, looping one leg over the chair's arm, sprawling like a teenager. Rolf lay down at her feet, but he kept his head up and his ears perked.

"You were right," Corky announced.

"About what?" she asked.

"Maggie. She's carrying Evan's accounts in her head."

"How could you possibly know that so fast?" Erin demanded, sitting forward.

"Trade secrets, love," he said.

"Though you probably use some of the same tricks in your interrogations," Carlyle said. "Don't get too excited. It's one thing to know she has the numbers; it's quite another to get them out of her head."

"But now we know our objective," Erin said. "We'll figure out a way to get her to talk."

"She loves Evan," Corky said.

"What?" Erin was astonished. "You mean... she *is* his mistress?"

"I can't believe I'm the one telling you this," Corky said. "But there's more than one kind of love, Erin. It's not always about the sex. Maggie's a misfit. She's never been able to relate well to other folk. Her mind works in a different way than yours or mine. Or Evan's, come to that. She had an unhappy childhood as a result."

"Everybody who ends up in the Mob had an unhappy childhood," Erin muttered.

"True enough," Corky said. "Her mum and da thought something was wrong with her. They took her to psychiatrists, tried to get her brain straightened out. They had her on medications, dreadful stuff that played silly buggers with her mind. You've noticed she's better than most at remembering things. Those drugs clouded her up, made her forgetful. It wasn't until she was eighteen or so that she got free of her kin and cleared up a bit. She says she scarce remembers her teenage years. It's all a black hole to her."

"Corky's been having a wee chat with Miss Callahan," Carlyle said. "Clearly."

"How did Evan find her?" Erin asked.

"By chance," Corky said. "This would be about fifteen years back. She'd taken a job as a file clerk in one of Evan's real-estate concerns. Her supervisor noticed she'd a knack for remembering things and happened to mention it to Evan. Next thing she knew, he'd taken her out to dinner and chatted her up. He paid for her college education and got her into Notre Dame in spite of her poor grades. He's the first lad to really appreciate what she can do, to make her feel special."

"So how did you find all this out from her?" Erin asked.

"I'm the second lad to make her feel special," he said, and Erin saw the flash of sadness in his eyes. "I'm holding you to our bargain, Erin. Whatever happens, Maggie's not to be harmed. She's not to go to prison. She's not even to testify in a courtroom."

"But she'll have to—" Erin began.

Carlyle laid a hand on her shoulder. "Her testimony would be valuable, sure enough," he said. "But do you really think she'd make a good witness on the stand? She'd look down at her own hands the whole time and the jury wouldn't even be able to hear her. She'll be more convincing on paper than she'd ever be in person."

"That's true," Erin said. "And believe me, I don't want any innocents getting hurt. I know she's worked for Evan, and she's technically a criminal, I guess, but... Christ, I just talked to a CEO today who tried to help his son cover up a murder. That's the sort of guy I want to get, not Maggie Callahan. She's just a bookkeeper."

"She's remarkable," Corky said. "And I'm going to help her."

"And you're not seducing her?" Erin asked, raising an eyebrow.

"I told you, that's off the table," Corky said. "You want to know how I opened her up? Fine! I told her some things about me and my childhood. I told her the truth about myself. I trusted her, so she trusted me. Trust isn't something she's had a lot of experience with, given the line of work we're both in. Are you bloody happy now?"

"Okay, okay," she said. "I didn't mean anything by that. It's just that this is a side of you I'm not used to seeing."

"Nay, he hides it with a fair degree of skill," Carlyle said. "But there's reasons I love this lad like a brother, darling. Or did you think I was such a poor judge of character?"

That question caught Erin by surprise. She felt herself getting flustered. "No!" she said. "I just thought... you know, he's been your best friend practically your whole life. We sometimes make allowances for old friends."

Corky grinned and winked at Carlyle. "She thought I was an utterly irredeemable rogue," he said. "And you were blind to my many and obvious faults simply because we looked out for one another when we were wee lads."

"That's not what I..." Erin began, then trailed off. It pretty much had been what she meant, and all three of them knew it. "You tried to sleep with my sister-in-law!" she added petulantly.

Corky shrugged in embarrassment. "Aye, that was a mistake," he said. "But I'm doing what I can to amend it. Doesn't that count for something?"

"Yeah, it does," Erin said. "But if you ever try it again, I'm going to shoot you."

He laughed.

"I'm not kidding," she said. "I Tased a guy in the nuts just a little while ago. You think I'm joking?"

"I know you're not," he said, still laughing. "That's why I love you, Erin."

"You're not as bad as you think you are," Erin replied. "And that's why I can never quite manage to hate you."

"Well, that's progress." Corky raised his glass. "Here's looking at all of us. May we live as long as we want..."

"And not want as long as we live," Carlyle finished. They knocked back their shots.

"And now I'm off," Corky said. "I'll get what you're needing, no fear."

"That's a load off our hearts," Carlyle said after the door swung shut behind Corky. "The end's in sight."

"Thank God for that," Erin said. She sagged back on the cushions. "You're going to think I'm crazy, but when you were in Chicago, I got really smashed."

"We're Irish, darling," he said. "I rather think other folk expect it of us."

"It's not funny," she said. "I got it in my head that Evan knew about us, about the whole operation, and he'd sent you out there with Finnegan to get rid of you. I thought I'd never see you again. I couldn't shut myself up, so I poured liquor into my brain until I blacked out."

"Nay," he said, looking at her with kind, concerned eyes. "It's not funny. You do know that's not how Evan would do for me, aye?"

"Yeah," she said. "He wouldn't take you to Chicago. He'd just have Snake Pritchard blow your brains out in some back alley and they'd dump you in the Jersey swamps. Is that supposed to make me feel better? That just means it could happen anytime. It could happen tomorrow; it could happen tonight."

"Nothing's certain in this life, darling." He took her hand and squeezed it. "Our respective lines of work are more dangerous than most, aye, but that's no guarantee of anything."

She sighed. "I know. I'm starting to understand Ian better, the way he's always on the edge. PTSD is fan-freaking-tastic."

"I can't tell you nothing's going to happen," he said. "God knows you've been up to your elbows in my blood in the past. But the bottle's no escape."

"I'm scared," she said with a bitter laugh. "I'm Erin O'Reilly. You know what the Mafia call me? Junkyard, as in junkyard dog. I'm a damn pit bull to them, but what if I'm more like a real pit bull? Tough on the outside, a marshmallow underneath? They're really sweet dogs, you know that? Most of them wouldn't hurt a fly. I thought I could handle this, but the uncertainty of it... how do you gangsters live? If I had to be one of you, I'd eat my own gun."

"Why do you think so many of us live the way Corky does?" he asked gently. "Day to day, no thought for the future? Erin, it was only once you gave me something worth living for that I started being afraid, and I'm more introspective than most."

"So that's the key? Have nothing to lose?"

He shook his head. "If you're living that way, you're half-dead already. Trust me. I've lived it. And trust Corky. He'll worm Evan's secrets out of Maggie. Then we'll arrest everyone and it'll be over."

"And I'll go back to chasing normal criminals all the time," she said. "Tasing frat boys and digging corpses out of concrete. This case was a real mess. I made a powerful enemy today."

"Another one? Grand." Carlyle smiled. "This calls for more whiskey, I'm thinking." He picked up the bottle.

"I should've arrested that boy's dad while I was at it," she said. "He knew about the murder, or guessed it. And he would've helped Chris make a run for it. You told me once there wasn't any line you wouldn't cross for the people you loved. You know what I learned today?"

"What's that, darling?" He refilled her glass.

"If you're going to be that way, you'd better be damn careful who you love," she said. "Because if you love the wrong person, they'll wreck your life along with theirs. Maybe I never should've fallen for you."

"You mean that?"

"Of course I don't." Erin took a drink. "Because that's the thing about love. You don't regret it, even when it makes you do stupid shit."

"Now there's words to live by," he said. "Here's a toast: to stupid, blind, mad love and all the things it makes us do. Here's to no regrets."

Erin clinked glasses with him. "And here's to making memories," she said. "So don't let me drink too much tonight, okay? I want to remember every good moment we have."

"I'll drink to that," Carlyle said. "But not too much."

They emptied their glasses. He took hers from her and set them down on the coffee table. "I'm sorry I worried you," he said.

"It wasn't your fault," she said.

"But your heart's my responsibility," he said. He laid his hand against her breastbone, feeling her heartbeat. "I'd best be taking good care of it. I love you, darling. You're my light and my life."

"And you're mine," she said, wrapping her hand around the back of his head and pulling him close. She kissed him, tasting the smoky whiskey that had been distilled in Glen Docherty-Kinlochewe, thousands of miles away. He was warm and he was here and he was *hers*, and that was all she asked. She let herself fall into the feeling, letting go of all the black fear and stress and tension.

They lay back on the couch, lips still locked together. Erin's fingers went to work on the buttons of Carlyle's shirt. His hands were on her shoulders, her back, caressing her.

"I got a tattoo," she murmured. "While I was drunk."

"Really?" He was surprised. "Of what? Where?"

She smiled, curling her lips against him. "I think I'll make you look for it."

"Now that's a fine idea, darling. I'd best make a detailed inspection."

He eased her blouse off her shoulders and kissed the exposed skin. She sighed and closed her eyes.

A cold, wet thing abruptly pushed against the side of her neck. Erin flinched and gasped in surprise, losing contact with

Carlyle. She turned her head and stared into Rolf's serious brown eyes.

"I'm a little busy here, kiddo," she said.

The Shepherd nudged her cheek with his astonishingly cold nose. He wagged his tail in a slow back-and-forth motion.

"What's the matter?" Carlyle asked, drawing back slightly.

"Supper," Erin groaned. "I forgot Rolf's supper."

Rolf's tail wagged faster. That was the right answer.

"I need to feed him," she said, sitting up and adjusting her blouse. "Can you hold that thought for a minute?"

Carlyle smiled. "I'll be right here."

"You promise?"

"I promise."

Here's a sneak peek from Book 18: Angel Face

Coming 12/12/22

Even if you were wearing a bulletproof vest, getting shot hurt. The bullet's energy, instead of traveling through your body, expended itself on the Kevlar weave of your body armor. The feeling was about the same as taking a full-force swing from a baseball bat. Paradoxically, wearing armor made you more likely to get knocked over, since the bullet wouldn't keep going. You might crack ribs, and you'd have one hell of a bruise.

The pain from a Taser was worse, but also more temporary. It was a deep, intense burning sensation that radiated out from the electrodes. Your muscles locked up and you couldn't move as long as the juice was flowing. But at least once it was over, you could get up and get on with your business. The only souvenir you'd carry would be a couple of little punctures and contact burns that would itch as they healed.

Even taking a punch was no picnic, not if the guy hitting you knew how to do it. A professional boxer's fist could shatter your jaw or knock you unconscious. Brain trauma could mess with just about everything upstairs, including motor functions, short-term and long-term memory, sensory input, and cognitive capacity. Concussions played hell with your faculties. You might get full use of your brain back, but you might not.

Erin O'Reilly had been punched in the head by a professional boxer. She'd also taken a Taser jolt, and had even been shot a couple of times. She liked to think she was tough, but she had no desire whatsoever to repeat any of those experiences. Still, given the choice, she might pick any of the three over the torture she was currently undergoing.

She tried not to squirm, not to give anything away. She was a trained police detective, experienced in interrogations. She looked down and to one side of the couch where she sat. Her partner Rolf sat bolt upright at her elbow, stern and serious. He returned her look and cocked his head questioningly. At a single word from her, he was ready to spring into action. He'd fight to the death to protect her. But he was no help here.

Erin sighed inwardly and forced herself to turn away from her K-9, back toward the matter at hand. If she could handle a high-speed car chase, an unexploded bomb, or an armed felon, she could deal with this.

"Now, here's Erin on her first day back from the hospital," Mary O'Reilly said, pointing to the photo album on the coffee table. "Look at that face. A perfect little angel. Isn't she just adorable?"

"Aye, she's a fine wee bairn," Morton Carlyle agreed. He was sandwiched between Erin and her mom on his living-room couch, upstairs from his pub. On the table in front of him, Erin's whole childhood was piled in three hefty albums. The three of them were currently looking at baby pictures.

"Her brother was so sweet," Mary went on, flipping the page to show a very young Sean O'Reilly Junior holding baby

Erin. "I swear, you could tell even at that age, Junior was going to be a doctor. I'm only surprised he didn't go into obstetrics."

Erin tried not to wince at the picture. In it, her face was scrunched up as if she was about to sneeze, scream, or possibly fill her diaper. Her eyes were squinting and her tiny mouth was open.

It wasn't that the pictures were so bad, all things considered. No, Mary O'Reilly's complete lack of subtlety was the really painful thing. Erin's mother had come down to the city, ostensibly to visit her grandchildren, Sean Junior and Michelle's two kids. But the O'Reilly matriarch had come to Manhattan armed with the albums, and Erin knew why.

Erin was thirty-six years old, never married, no kids. She'd been seeing Carlyle since New Year's, over nine months now, and had been living with him for almost half that time. In Mary's books, that meant it was time to start thinking marriage and children, the more and the sooner the better.

Accordingly, Erin's mom was mounting a full-court press. She probably thought she was being delicate and polite. And Erin supposed, compared to Carlyle's business associates, she was. But then, those associates were the O'Malley Irish Mob, a motley crew of murderous thugs, racketeers, and smugglers. Their idea of subtlety involved back alleys and tire irons. It was a low bar to clear.

The worst part of it was, Erin didn't need to be convinced. She liked kids, adored her niece and nephew, and was completely on board with the idea of having her own one of these days. But not yet, and she couldn't explain her hesitation to her mom. Mary O'Reilly thought Carlyle was an ordinary publican, a well-to-do gentleman who'd made his money as a successful small-business owner. But Carlyle had two secrets.

The first secret, widely known in the New York underworld, was that the Barley Corner, in addition to being a thriving watering hole for blue-collar Irishmen, was also a front for the O'Malleys, a money-laundering operation, and a haven for sports bookies. The second, known to fewer than ten people, was that Carlyle had turned informant and was compiling information to use against his boss Evan O'Malley. He'd made the choice out of love for Erin, desperation after a near-fatal shooting, and the long-shot hope of personal redemption.

Mary O'Reilly could probably forgive Carlyle his shady past. But she didn't know how much danger he and Erin were currently in. Until they'd brought down the O'Malleys and could go for a drive without needing to check the underside of Carlyle's Mercedes for car bombs, marriage and children were off the table. And they couldn't tell her this, because Mary was a generous, loving, open-hearted woman who didn't know how to keep her mouth shut.

So Erin was doomed to suffer through an interminable morning of thinly-veiled hints about the joys of motherhood, her mom thinking Erin was dragging her feet while her biological clock ticked down toward zero.

Erin glanced at the living-room clock and unclenched her jaw. She slipped her hand out of Carlyle's and stood. Carlyle, ever the gentleman, also got to his feet.

"Sorry, Mom," she lied, following it up with the truth. "I have an appointment. Work."

"I thought you were off duty today," Mary said.

"I am. But I need to be in court. There's an arraignment, a Mafia guy, and I was one of the arresting officers."

"Mattie Madonna's lad?" Carlyle said. "Alfredo?"

"You know a Mafia goon?" Mary asked.

"I knew his father, some years back," Carlyle said smoothly. "I'd hardly call us friends, but we were acquainted with some of the same people. I'd heard the lad was in a wee bit of trouble."

"Parole violation," Erin said. "I promised his dad I'd look in on him, see what I could do for him. Sorry to run out on you like this."

"And we haven't even gotten to her grade school pictures yet," Mary said, pouting a little.

"I'm going nowhere, Mrs. O'Reilly," Carlyle said. "I'd be happy to see more of what Erin was like as a wee lass."

Erin shot him a grateful look and made for the exit. Rolf bounded alongside, tail wagging. The German Shepherd didn't understand why humans made such a point of sitting indoors all the time when they could be running around outdoors. The world was full of bad guys to chase, smells to investigate, and rubber toys to chew on. It was time to get out there and patrol their territory.

"Sorry, kiddo," she told him at the top of the stairs. "We can't have you in the courtroom. The lawyers would call it intimidation. *Bleib*."

Rolf froze, one paw raised. He couldn't believe it. His partner was going on adventures and he couldn't come. He gave it a moment, seeing if the instructions changed, but Erin turned away. Rolf was a good boy, so he stayed put, as instructed, but he gave her a reproachful stare as only a dog could. His intense brown eyes bored holes in Erin's back as she fled down the stairs and out of the apartment.

* * *

Erin didn't like going to court. As far as she was concerned, her role in the legal system was to collect evidence, arrest the perps, and hand them over to the District Attorney. After that, they became his problem. Erin distrusted lawyers, even prosecutors, and found courtroom proceedings incredibly boring. She also knew that sometimes guilty guys got off the hook, and there was nothing she could do about it, which was doubly infuriating. Being a detective had enough frustrations without that, so she steered clear of trials unless called on to testify.

But today was different. It wasn't just an excuse to get away from her mother's baby blitz. She'd made a promise to a dying man that she'd try to help his son. Matthew Madonna might have been a drug-dealing Mafioso who'd gone down in a hail of bullets in a seedy bar, and his son Alfredo was cut from the same cloth, but Erin had held Mattie's hand as he died. If they hadn't been friends, they'd shared an enemy: Vincenzo Moreno, new don of the Lucarelli Family. Vinnie had been behind Madonna's murder, along with several others, but Erin hadn't been able to prove it. Vinnie's nickname was "The Oil Man," and he'd proved as slippery as ever. Vinnie had slithered out of trouble and Alfie had ended up fatherless and incarcerated.

Erin parked her Charger in one of the police spaces at the courthouse. She went through the front doors and the security checkpoint, where she showed her gold shield and handed over both her sidearm and her backup ankle gun. It struck her as a little silly that she, a decorated NYPD detective, wasn't allowed to bring a gun into court, but the men hired by the US Marshals to provide security were. She submitted as gracefully as she could. However, being unarmed left her very nervous these days, particularly without her dog.

The day's proceedings were ludicrous. An arraignment wasn't a trial. A jury wasn't going to be there. All it consisted of was the formal reading of the charges against the defendant and that defendant entering his plea. The whole thing would only take a few minutes.

Alfredo Madonna should have been arraigned within twenty-four hours of being charged. That was the rules. However, in Madonna's case, there'd been a delay. The kid had been hospitalized. It seemed Madonna had eaten something that had disagreed with him, badly enough that he'd needed to have his stomach pumped. Erin had been distracted at the time, dealing with a budding serial killer, and he hadn't technically been her prisoner, so she'd only gotten the information at second hand, days later.

Sergeant Logan, a Street Narcotics cop at the Five, had called her just last night to let her know the score. Logan was a good guy and a rock-solid street officer, a friend who'd helped Erin on several occasions. It was his squad that had officially taken Madonna in.

"Our buddy Alfie almost died in custody," Logan told her.

"What?" Erin exclaimed. "How? When?"

"Seems he had an allergic reaction to his dinner his first night in jail," Logan said. "A pretty bad one. Landed him in the hospital, but he pulled through okay. They're putting him in front of a judge tomorrow, now that he can stand up under his own power."

And that was why Erin was here now. She wanted to see Alfredo Madonna, and hopefully find out what had happened to him. She suspected Vinnie's hand, but then, she suspected Vinnie of everything connected with the Lucarellis. The bastard had somehow managed to have a man killed in the middle of Erin's own beloved Eightball, right there in the holding cells. If he could do that, he could definitely have slipped Alfie something nasty to go with his supper. The only surprise was that the kid was still breathing.

Erin was gratified to see a grim-looking Deputy Marshal outside the courtroom, keeping an eye on the corridor. He gave her a cool once-over, examined her credentials, and stepped aside.

The courtroom was nearly empty. Arraignments were public, so in theory anybody could show up, but except in high-profile cases they were not well-attended functions. There was the judge, the court recorder, the prosecutor, the defendant, and the defendant's legal team. Erin had arrived a little early, so the only people in the room yet were the bailiff and the prosecutor.

Erin eyed the young man at the front of the room. The DA's guy was just a kid, probably some wet-behind-the-ears law school graduate on his first case. It ought to be a slam-dunk. Alfie Madonna was on parole, prohibited from associating with known felons and from carrying firearms. He'd been found in the presence of several men with long criminal records, some of whom had been dead, in close proximity to a revolver, recently fired, covered with his fingerprints. Though Alfie's dad had sworn to Erin in his dying declaration that he'd been the one to kill all the other men who'd died in that room, Alfie had still been charged with second-degree murder in addition to the weapons and parole violations. He was looking at a big pile of years.

Erin sat a few rows back and waited. She didn't have to wait long; only a few minutes later, the doors swung open and Alfie Madonna walked in, flanked by his lawyer on one side and a square-jawed Deputy on the other. Erin recognized the lawyer; Kingston Schultz, an attorney of Jamaican extraction who'd been representing Alfie and his dad for years. The lawyer had his arm around his client, helping him down the aisle.

Alfie looked rough. He was pale and hollow-eyed, like a man who'd seen a ghost. But he walked with slow, deliberate purpose, hardly leaning on his lawyer. He looked straight ahead, not seeming to notice Erin. The expression on his face was cold and determined.

Once the defendant and his lawyer were seated, the bailiff stepped to the door behind the lectern. A moment later, the judge emerged. He was a gray-haired man, magisterial in his black robe. The few people in the room got to their feet when he entered, then sat right back down again.

The judge droned out the necessary legal boilerplate. Before he'd finished his first sentence, Erin could already feel her eyes starting to glaze over. After he'd finished, the prosecutor got up and read the charges. Erin already knew what these were, so she let them slide past her ears. She was watching Alfie. The kid was obviously still very weak, but he was showing some grit, refusing to so much as slouch in his chair. Erin really wanted to go right up to him and start asking questions, but she didn't want to get tackled by the bailiff, so she resisted the impulse.

"Mr. Madonna," the judge said. "You've heard the state's charges. How do you plead?"

"Your Honor," Schultz said, speaking on Alfie's behalf. "The defense moves that the charge of murder be dropped. The State's case is weak, undermined by the confession of Matthew Madonna. The state has produced no conclusive evidence that my client fired any shots during the fracas at Lucia's Bar."

The judge turned his eyes on the prosecutor.

"Your Honor," the kid said. "The State agrees to drop the charge of second-degree murder."

Erin was suddenly wide awake, sitting forward on the edge of her bench. Just like that, they were throwing away the most serious charge? Without even trying for a plea bargain? She didn't think the case was weak at all. Men had gone to prison on shakier evidence. What was going on here?

"To the remaining charges," Schultz said, "my client pleads *nolo contendere.*"

Erin didn't know Latin, but she knew that phrase. It meant "no contest," and it was a lawyerly way of admitting guilt without explicitly admitting it. This case wouldn't go to trial. Now all that was left was for the judge to set bail prior to sentencing.

"Very well," the judge said. "Defendant is released on recognizance, to appear for sentencing two weeks from today." He banged his gavel on the lectern, stood up, and left the room.

Erin was stunned. The judge hadn't thrown Alfie back in a cell, hadn't even bothered to set bail. That was beyond absurd. Alfie Madonna was a repeat offender, a career criminal. If the murder charge had remained in effect, he might have been held without bail at all, or the judge might have set a prohibitively high bond. But now Alfie could just walk out of the courthouse and go home to await his sentencing.

Somebody had put a thumb on the scales of justice, Erin was sure of it. What she didn't know was who and why. But she intended to find out.

Ready for more?

Join Steven Henry's author email list
for the latest on new releases, upcoming books and
series, behind-the-scenes details, events, and more.

Be the first to know about new releases in the Erin
O'Reilly Mysteries by signing up at
tinyurl.com/StevenHenryEmail

About the Author

Steven Henry learned how to read almost before he learned how to walk. Ever since he began reading stories, he wanted to put his own on the page. He lives a very quiet and ordinary life in Minnesota with his wife and dog.

Also by Steven Henry

Ember of Dreams
The Clarion Chronicles, Book One

When magic awakens a long-forgotten folk, a noble lady, a young apprentice, and a solitary blacksmith band together to prevent war and seek understanding between humans and elves.

Lady Kristyn Tremayne – An otherwise unremarkable young lady's open heart and inquisitive mind reveal a hidden world of magic.

Robert Blackford – A humble harp maker's apprentice dreams of being a hero.

Master Gabriel Zane – A master blacksmith's pursuit of perfection leads him to craft an enchanted sword, drawing him out of his isolation and far from his cozy home.

Lord Luthor Carnarvon – A lonely nobleman with a dark past has won the heart of Kristyn's mother, but at what cost?

Readers love *Ember of Dreams*

"The more I got to know the characters, the more I liked them. The female lead in particular is a treat to accompany on her journey from ordinary to extraordinary."

"The author's deep understanding of his protagonists' motivations and keen eye for psychological detail make Robert and his companions a likable and memorable cast."

Learn more at tinyurl.com/emberofdreams.

More great titles from Clickworks Press

www.clickworkspress.com

The Altered Wake
Megan Morgan

Amid growing unrest, a family secret and an ancient laboratory unleash long-hidden superhuman abilities. Now newly-promoted Sentinel Cameron Kardell must chase down a rogue superhuman who holds the key to the powers' origin: the greatest threat Cotarion has seen in centuries – and Cam's best friend.

"Incredible. Starts out gripping and keeps getting better."

Learn more at clickworkspress.com/sentinel1.

Hubris Towers: The Complete First Season
Ben Y. Faroe & Bill Hoard

Comedy of manners meets comedy of errors in a new series for fans of Fawlty Towers and P. G. Wodehouse.

"So funny and endearing"

"Had me laughing so hard that I had to put it down to catch my breath"

"Astoundingly, outrageously funny!"

Learn more at clickworkspress.com/hts01.

Death's Dream Kingdom
Gabriel Blanchard

A young woman of Victorian London has been transformed into a vampire. Can she survive the world of the immortal dead—or perhaps, escape it?

"The wit and humor are as Victorian as the setting... a winsomely vulnerable and tremendously crafted work of art."

"A dramatic, engaging novel which explores themes of death, love, damnation, and redemption."

Learn more at clickworkspress.com/ddk.

Share the love!

Join our microlending team at
kiva.org/team/clickworkspress.

Keep in touch!

Join the Clickworks Press email list
and get freebies, production updates, special deals,
behind-the-scenes sneak peeks, and more.

Sign up today at clickworkspress.com/join.